KFIR
LUZZATTO

Crossing the
Meadow

Pine Ten, LLC
205 N Michigan Avenue
Chicago, ILL 60601

Fist published by Echelon Press 2003

ISBN: 978-1938212017

Books by Kfir Luzzatto:

CROSSING THE MEADOW

THE ODYSSEY GENE

THE EVELYN PROJECT

HAVE BOOK, WILL TRAVEL (With Yonatan Luzzatto)

AN ITALIAN OBSESSION

EXODUS '95

CHIPLESS

ONCE AWAKENED

The Tessa Extra-Sensory Agent series:

TESSA (Tessa Extra-Sensory Agent Book 1)

THE OTHERS (Tessa Extra-Sensory Agent Book 2)

HUNTER (Tessa Extra-Sensory Agent Book 3)

The DEAD & BUSY series

#1: ACCIDENTAL LAZARUS

#2: PHANTOM LOVER

#3: MICE

#4: THE ACCOUNTANT

Contents

CHAPTER I: *The Fog* *1*

CHAPTER II: *About Town* *10*

CHAPTER III: *Discovery* *18*

CHAPTER IV: *The Tram* *28*

CHAPTER V: *Uncle Henry* *38*

CHAPTER VI: *The League* *46*

CHAPTER VII: *The Museum* *57*

CHAPTER VIII: *The Family* *69*

CHAPTER IX: *The Park* *79*

CHAPTER X: *The Apartment* *88*

CHAPTER XI: *Friends* *99*

CHAPTER XII: *The Teacher* *111*

CHAPTER XIII: *David* *122*

CHAPTER XIV: *Building an Interest* *133*

CHAPTER XV: *Finding Clues* *145*

CHAPTER XVI: *Exasperating David* *158*

CHAPTER XVII: *Investigating* *170*

CHAPTER XVIII: *A Lucky Break* *182*

CHAPTER XIX: *Shopping?* *194*

CHAPTER XX: *Letting Go* *207*

Meet the Author *218*

CHAPTER I
The Fog

"Friend of yours?"

George looked at the girl who had spoken, as if surprised to see her there, sitting at the table with him. Lost in a reverie, running in his head through the events that had brought him here, to this small café, he'd been sitting there for a long time now, looking through the window into the thick fog, and trying to force his eyes to see the entrance to the place that once had been his home.

Many years had passed since his father, a man of comfortable means, had moved his commercial interests to the United States of America, taking with him his wife and his adolescent son.

He could certainly not complain. At forty-five lived a comfortable life and provided handsomely for his little family–his beloved wife Jane, and Sharon, the teenage girl they both adored–with a small business that practically ran itself. He would have lived a uniformly peaceful life, but for the dream.

The dream–or rather, the nightmare–had begun many years ago. It was a short one, but no less frightening for that. In the dream, he stooped on his knees in the bathroom of his home, helping someone whose face he could not see, to fill the void beneath the bathtub with sand. The rest of the space, he knew, was taken up by the body of a woman, whom he was helping to bury. Although he never saw the woman clearly in the dream, he knew with absolute certainty that she was there. The exasperating part of it was that he always woke up, often in a sweat, knowing that the meaning of the dream was about to become clear to him, in a manner that would make it look perfectly rational.

He'd had many other nightmares over the years, some of them recurring at various frequencies. However, this particular one carried a special quality of reality that he did not sense in all other dreams, and that had remained unblemished for decades. At last, he had come to the realization that there was no way to exorcise the spell, other than to go back to his old neighborhood. But now that he was here, he didn't know what to do.

The girl seated at the little round table near the window had attracted his attention. She was looking around with uninterested, yet deep black eyes. She was small and young– maybe twenty-two or twenty-three years old–with chestnut hair fastened into a wavy pigtail, and an evening dress unsuitable for the cold evening weather of the early fall. He had been looking at her for a while, almost hypnotized by her elegant figure. He didn't think that she had noticed him. But he could not take his eyes off her; how fragile she seemed. He wondered what she was doing there all alone.

Time passed without her giving any sign of leaving. It looked as if whomever it was that she was waiting for, had stood her up. Quite a jerk, he must be, letting such a nice girl wait.

He hadn't had a real conversation with anybody for too long now, and had started to feel lonesome. He resolved to approach her and, having built up the courage to do so, got up and walked slowly to her table.

"May I join you, *Signorina*?" he asked.

She looked up briefly, barely taking the time to size him. "Please do," she answered, looking back at the tablecloth again, without any display of interest, or show of surprise.

He sat down and hesitated for a few moments before speaking. "I saw you looking out of the window at that building," he started out apologetically, "and I wondered–I lived there as a child."

"You did?" she asked, without managing to show surprise, or an interest. "You sound like a foreigner, though."

"I have been abroad for over thirty years now. I guess that makes me sound a little funny. Tell me, if it is not too rude of me to ask, what are you doing out here at night? This is not a place for a nice girl like you, and may be dangerous too. It used to be crowded and busy here, when I was young, but now–"

For a moment the room seemed transformed, as he recalled the way it had been. There, behind that bench, stood the pizza man, turning small dough balls into flat pizza bases. He had always admired the way the *Pizzaiolo*, as they used to call him, performed his magic by turning the dough in the air between the palms of his hands, until the small ball became a flat, thin plate. And for a moment he had a vision of the oven just behind him, now gone, from which the *Pizzaiolo* withdrew gorgeous pizzas dripping with mozzarella cheese; the scene came alive in his mind for a moment, only to vanish immediately again.

The laughter of the once light-hearted couples that filled the room and turned it into a warm sanctuary, faded away quickly as they had arisen in his head, leaving them again in the cold atmosphere that the street window cast upon their table.

"I am sorry," he said, "I let my mind wander. You were saying?"

"I was asking if he is a friend of yours," she said, looking at the window beside them.

George turned to his right, following her amused gaze, and gaped at the window in astonishment. A man was standing outside, a few inches from him, his face pressed to the window. He looked familiar.

"He–he looks like my Uncle Henry," George said slowly. "But, of course, he can't be him. Uncle Henry died many years ago."

"A relative, perhaps?" said the girl.

"No, no. He had no relatives other than my mother," he said in a murmur, brushing the notion aside. The man was standing, motionless, staring at George, with his right hand above his eyes, apparently in an attempt to shade whatever little light came from the inside. George was staring back, unable to decide how to react.

"But what does he want? Why is he staring at me like this?"

The man now stepped back from the glass window, smiling, waved a hand at George in a saluting motion, turned around, and quickly disappeared into the fog. George was rattled. He had been very fond of his Uncle Henry, who had died shortly before they left the country, and facing what seemed to be his twin brother, suddenly like this, brought back forgotten and painful memories.

"I'm glad he's gone," George said quietly, almost to himself.

He turned back to the girl, making an effort to act his composed self again.

"I apologize for my behavior. You will think me rude. I have been sitting here without introducing myself. My name is George, and you are?"

"I'm Clara, and I didn't think you rude. A little strange, perhaps," she said, smiling reassuringly, "but clearly not rude."

"I'm glad," he said, smiling back. "So, what are you doing here all alone, at this time of night?"

"Well, this is my zone."

"I'm not sure that I understand," he said, "what do you mean by 'my zone'?"

A light of amusement passed through her eyes–she had beautiful, lively eyes. His own gaze was riveted to her graceful round face, and he could not bring himself to look away. *I am only having an innocent conversation to while away the time a bit. Nothing to be ashamed of,* he reassured himself.

"I mean that this is where I meet my clients," she said, still amused, "old and new. Here is where I sit, always. Men can come to me, just as you did, and become acquainted. Then, if it so pleases me, we become friends." She evidently saw no light of comprehension in his eyes and added, quite simply, "I am a prostitute. This is where I pick up men. Then we go elsewhere and, if the price is right, I spend the night with them."

George got up quickly, almost instinctively.

"Sit down!" she ordered him, as he hurriedly started to

move away from her. "I didn't plan for you to be a client. And I didn't think you were planning it either."

"I–I apologize for my reaction," he said, sitting down again. "I didn't mean to be rude. It's just that I never–I didn't–"

"I understand. You never met a *puttana*. Well, look, I don't bite. I'm clean and I'm kind," she said, counting with her fingers. "I believe you may find me to be a suitable partner for conversation." The irony in her voice was stinging, particularly since the amused look would not leave her eyes.

"Can we start this all over again, please?" he asked, mortified. Then, encouraged by her silence he continued, "Tell me about yourself."

"There isn't much to tell. And I am not in the mood," she said curtly. "You tell me about yourself."

"Oh, I'm a very boring person. I own a small business back in the USA, which is doing quite well on its own, and this is how I can afford to get away. I've come back to revisit my childhood neighborhood. You know, I was born just a few kilometers from here, and I lived in the house in front, on the fifth floor, until I left."

"Family?"

"I'm married with one daughter–Sharon. She is seventeen now, and beautiful."

"I noticed the wedding band. Are you happily married?"

"Yes, I am."

"Do you think she is missing you now?"

What a strange question, he thought. "I would be surprised if Jane didn't miss me," he said. "We've never been apart for long before. Why shouldn't she?"

"Oh, I thought maybe–"

"What?"

"Nothing. Forget it. So why are you here?"

He suppressed an urge to tell her about his dream and the real reason why he was here. After all, she was a total stranger who should be justified in thinking him mad to undertake such a trip on account of a nightmare.

"I have come to revisit the streets of my youth, you could say," he said guardedly.

"And how do you find it?"

"The neighborhood, you mean?" She nodded slightly (she had a way of cocking her head to one side that invoked intimacy), and he continued, "Well, I don't know. It's kind of strange. On the one hand, I know every stone around here, and very little has changed since those days; but on the other, I don't seem to recognize anybody.

"I walked near my old school one morning, and I found my name scratched on the fence, just where I used to stand waiting for the gates to open in the morning, when I was seven or eight years old. Nobody has bothered to paint or plaster it. I saw the names of many other boys from those days, written around the neighborhood. I think I recall the faces of some of them, but then, my memory could be playing tricks on me. I've been walking around, trying to match those childish faces to people around here, as they are now. I think I may have spotted one or two of my old classmates, but I wasn't sure enough to walk up to them and introduce myself. And then even if I did, what would I say next?"

He didn't tell her of his one attempt to do so. It was while he stood at the entrance of a department store he used to visit as a child, debating whether to go inside and see how it had changed, that he had spotted someone he knew well from his school days, coming out of the shop.

"Hi, old boy!" he had called to him, putting out a hand for him to shake, but his old friend had gone straight ahead, as if not seeing him, and would have trampled over him, had he not moved aside quickly enough. It had made him feel pretty silly.

"So what are your plans?" she asked.

"To tell you the truth," he said, "I'm not sure what I want to do next."

"It seems to me that you are making a very poor job of your visit," she said, looking at him with mocking eyes. "Didn't you make any plans at all before you came here?"

"Actually, I acted on an impulse. It felt right that I should visit here, and so I came, without planning ahead." The truth of this fact had only just dawned on him. He actually had no plan at all, except for the very general idea of getting to the roots of his nightmare.

"For one thing, I just feel like walking around to make my peace with the streets of my childhood." He had never before thought of his drive to return to his birthplace in those terms. He now felt as if he owed these streets an apology–for leaving them so suddenly, for not having said goodbye in a proper way, and perhaps for not having given a thought to them for so long.

"Then why are you wasting your time sitting here, staring at this old building?" she asked. "Shouldn't you be out there instead?"

"You know, I wish I could visit my old apartment. I would like to stay for a while and let my mind go back to when I was a child. But I don't think that its present occupants would agree."

"I'll tell you what I'll do for you," she said. "I'll take you around to see the streets and what's in them. I can show you things. I know my way around here."

Her hand was in his, and she was on her feet. He didn't know why, but he knew he could trust her.

"Thank you. I'd like that," he said, gratefully. "I do feel a little lost."

"Okay. Now, just hold my hand and don't let go. I don't want to lose you in the fog."

He left with her through the main door, and they were outside, blending in the milky white mist. Suddenly he realized that he had not paid his bill. Then, he recalled, he had not ordered anything, and neither had she. Moreover, the waitress had not asked for their orders either.

CHAPTER II
About Town

They were walking side by side, without touching. The fog had lifted a little now, and it was easier to see the silhouettes of the buildings around them. The street they were walking in was wide and punctuated with chestnut trees, and their broad yellow leaves piled on the ground, creating a natural carpet.

A telephone booth stood at the corner of a street, and he suddenly felt the urge to call home.

"Would you mind if I took a few minutes to make a phone call?" he asked.

"Not at all. Go ahead. I'll sit over there," she said, pointing at a wooden bench between two nearby trees.

"I'll be quick," he promised. He got into the booth, closed the door, and prepared to dial a familiar number.

The receiver was stuck. George cursed it silently and tried with all his strength to lift it, but something was holding it in its cradle. The lighting in the booth was bad and he tried in vain to discover what the problem might be. With a final effort he managed to rotate the microphone a little toward him and apparently also to dislodge the receiver from its place in the cradle, slightly but enough to obtain a dial tone. He would have to put his face next to the receiver–a ridiculous position to assume for a telephone conversation–but the alternative was to look for another booth and he was already anxious to speak with his family; and Clara might become tired of waiting.

He dialed quickly and after a few seconds someone picked up the phone at his home. His daughter's voice, coming from the other end of the line, was a delight to him, as always.

"Hello, honey! How are you doing?"

He was relieved that, at last, he had been able to communicate. His previous experience had been very frustrating. Every time he had to wait for the dial tone, after which he would only obtain a frustrating series of clicks, rings and echoes, which always announced the forthcoming death of the line. But this time, he seemed to have gotten lucky. He had heard the friendly ring of his home telephone within seconds. At last, he thought, the phone is working properly.

"Do you hear me?" his daughter was shouting.

The telephone lines have never been so bad, he thought. "I have a bad connection," he shouted. "I'll speak slowly."

"Are you listening to me, you creep?" she was shouting. "This is the last time that you call me today and make noises at me over the telephone. I am having all calls traced by the police. You hear me?" Her voice was almost hysterical, and she finally hung up.

He stood in the booth, feeling helpless. He was anxious to

call her back and reassure her that it was only a bad connection, and not a sex maniac calling her. He dialed the number again, and this time he heard the immediate click of the answering machine. She appeared to have had enough of creeps for the day.

"Hi! Mom and I are out, but you can leave a message at the beep," said his daughter's recorded voice. "And don't forget to leave your name and a number so that we can call you back."

He realized with a twinge of pain that the message had been changed since he'd left for his trip, and hung-up. He didn't like his family doing things without him, particularly if the things they did excluded him. It had happened to him every now and then, and it was only natural that this should be so in a house with two women who had in common things they were unable to share with him. Nevertheless, he thought, they shouldn't have changed the message so soon. There was no point in trying to call her again now, anyway. She was certainly going to leave the machine on until she felt the "creep" was frustrated enough to give up.

He lifted his head, sensing that he was not alone. Outside the booth stood the man from the café, his eyes level with his, gazing intently into George's face. George started, then shivered. At close distance, this man looked very much like Uncle Henry, as he remembered him from his childhood days. The man's behavior, however, was inexcusable. Whatever the reason for this persecution, George was not going to stand for it. He opened the door of the booth and stepped out, ready to confront the stranger. He was gone. Could it be that he had dreamed him up? He was overexcited, but still the man had looked real to him.

"Clara," he called urgently.

"I'm here," she said, walking quickly toward him. "Have

you finished?"

Did you see that man?"

"What man?"

"The one who stared at me through the café window. He was here again. Have you seen him?"

"No. I've seen no one. I don't think there was anybody around here," she looked at him and continued, you're obviously nervous. I hope it's not because of me. Come on, let's keep walking. It'll be good for you."

They continued along the boulevard that ended in a meadow–a small park, he assumed, since this area of the city had never been very lavish in green areas. A large monument stood on the grass, commemorating an unidentified general on his war-horse. Water poured from the horse's mouth into a basin, next to which a marble inscription listed names and dates, those of long-forgotten heroes who had given their lives for their country.

They sat on a nearby bench for a long minute, watching the flowing water, almost hypnotized by the sound it made hitting the wet stone.

"Listen," she said suddenly. "Can you hear the wind playing among the treetops? They tell me that there is no other place in the world where you can hear such a distinctive sound."

He listened for a while. "It sounds like any other place to me," he said.

"I haven't heard the wind singing in the trees anywhere else, so I can't compare," she said. "Still, it always reminds me of a story they used to tell me as a child, about the origin of this sound.

"The way the story goes, God appears in a dream to a poor man who lives here, and tells him, 'I am ordering you to get up and head north, until you come to the mountains. There you will pick a flower that you will recognize by its smell, and will bring it back here. Once you plant it in your garden, you will become the wealthiest man in town.'

"And he tells God, 'God Almighty, I would like nothing better than do what Thou hast ordered, but how am I to know that I have reached the mountains, when I am blind and cannot see them?'

'You will know that you have reached the mountains,' said God, 'when your strength will not suffice to keep you going on the steep path. Then you will find yourself in a bed of flowers where you will pick the one, which has the strongest scent.'

'But, My Lord, how will I know that I got back here, and that I am not in some other city, when I am mute and cannot speak to ask my way? '

'Listen to this sound, ' said The Lord. 'This is the sound of the wind in the treetops of your city. There is no other sound like it in the entire world, and there will never be. And when you hear this sound again, you will know that you have returned to this city, and you will plant the flower in this city and will live happily thereafter.'

"And this, according to the old legend, is how this sound was created."

"And how did the story end?" he asked. "Did the old man become wealthy?"

"Well, no. He found the mountains all right, but then he fell off a cliff and got killed. So probably, it was not God in his dream, after all. Still, the city got its distinctive sound."

They sat quietly for a while, brooding on the tale and its significance. No matter how hard he tried, he could not work out how it was meant to enrich and educate you, except perhaps that it taught you to trust nobody. Or perhaps it meant that you should double-check who you are talking to, and never take anybody's identity at face value. Still, it was a good story, he thought.

Another sound reached him now. Someone was sobbing. He walked quickly to the other side of the monument. A child was sitting on the ground, weeping. He was perhaps ten years old, and was alone. "Get up, my boy," said George, "and tell me what's the matter."

"Sir, oh sir," said the boy in a whimper. "I can't find my parents, and I'm lost. I don't know what to do."

"What happened?" he asked. "When did you last see your parents?"

"We were driving in our car...we were going to visit my grandma, and suddenly there was a crash." The child was still crying while talking, but the presence of a benevolent grown-up seemed to be reassuring him. "I think that a bus hit the side of our car, but I don't remember much. I woke up here and I don't know where I am. I don't know my way home. Where is my Nanny? Have you seen my Nanny?" he asked, weeping again.

Clara had caught up with them now, and touched his arm. "Let me talk to him," she said, "I have a way with children, and I know what to do to calm him down."

She turned to the child, took his hand in hers, and moved aside, whispering apparently soothing words in his ears, because after a few seconds they were absorbed in lively conversation. He could not hear what they were saying, but it was apparent that she was saying the right things. The child was asking questions and seemed to like the answers; he even thought at one point that the poor child was smiling.

He walked the short distance to them, and addressed her, "We must take care of this child, and help him find his parents. Let's go!"

"No," she said. "Look—"

He turned around, following her gaze, to see an old lady walking on the grass toward them. She wore a cloak and a hat so old-fashioned that he had only seen similar ones in movies. She was thin and her face was hawk-like, and yet she emanated strength and purposefulness. She stood beside them and put a hand on the child's shoulder.

"I will take this from here. Thank you," she said, looking at nobody in particular.

"But, what? And who?" he started to argue, but his eyes then fell on the child. He was clearly happy and secure now. He realized then that this must be the nanny.

"Well, miss," he said. "I think that you should report what happened here to the authorities. I'm only a tourist myself, but am sure that they would want to know that a child has been terrorized here—even if it means an inquiry into how he happened to be left alone for such a long time." He looked for approval on the nanny's stern face, but his gaze only met the same inexpressive look.

"No doubt the whole matter has been dealt with, and should be construed as having been considered with the utmost attention and care, and due steps having been taken such that it can be properly concluded," she said, almost without moving her lips, and turned around, without another word, walking away from them.

"What did she *say*?" he asked, talking more to himself than to the others.

The child waved his hand in farewell and he and the nanny walked together on the grass, away from them, until they disappeared in the fog.

"All's well that ends well," said he.

"Yes," she agreed; "he is happy now, and in peace. He deserves it, being so young."

"Let's walk back now," he said. There was nothing more to keep them there. They walked in silence, enjoying the music played by the wind in the treetops, and the feeling of the yellow carpet of leaves. He had never had much time for strolling around, during the last few years. Most of his time had been devoted to his work. Having a lot of free time on his hands was a new experience to him. He promised himself to learn to enjoy it.

CHAPTER III
Discovery

George was standing by the window, looking out, when he sensed Clara's presence behind him. He had been longing to see her from the moment that they had parted company, after walking back from the meadow, and he had realized, too late, that he had forgotten to ask her where she lived. He had been afraid that he might not see her again, and was relieved now to see her graceful figure walking quickly toward him.

"Gosh, am I glad to see you!" he said. "There are a thousand things that I need to ask you."

"Like what?" she asked, standing in front of him and eyeing him seriously.

"Well, there are these strange things that have been happening to me since I got here. At first, I thought that I was misinterpreting them on account of my being practically a stranger around here; but then I started to think about different incidents, and I don't know what to make of them. I'm sorry to bother you with this, but you are the only person I know in this city. I hope you won't think me a nut, or something."

"I promise I won't," she said softly. "Go ahead, tell me."

"Well, for one, I don't seem to be able to call home. I have tried calling my wife and my daughter several times, but I can't get through to them–or to anybody else, for that matter. I have tried talking to the operator, but that didn't get me anywhere either. If this were a communist country, I would be ready to swear that the secret police is blocking my calls. Being as it is, I don't know. But there must be a conspiracy going on here. All this can't be a coincidence."

"And what else?" she prompted him.

"Well." He hesitated, "I don't know if I should be telling you this–you'll think that I am stark raving mad–but I think that people I know from back then, have been instructed not to talk to me. I have run into a number of people I recognized, but when I approached them they invariably just looked through me, as if I didn't exist, and went on without answering me. One case could be someone really not recognizing me, but after the third and the fourth time, I am pretty sure that there must be a guiding hand behind all this. I don't know what the purpose is, and who's going to the trouble of staging all this for my benefit, but I can't ignore the facts. And it's getting pretty scary, you know."

"And this hasn't suggested anything to you?" she asked.

"That's what I'm telling you. I don't know what to make of it. Do you?"

"We must talk," she said curtly, steering him toward a bench in a quiet corner of the room. "Come, sit beside me."

He looked at her, surprised by the somber tone of her voice and the sadness in her eyes. She took a long breath and continued, almost in a murmur, "God, I wish I weren't the one to tell you."

"Tell me what? What are you talking about?"

"What's today's date?"

"Well, it's–uh–I haven't checked today. I've sort of lost track of time since I got here."

"Then tell me the name of the hotel where you are staying."

He couldn't see what all this had to do with what he was asking, but was willing to humor her, for a while at least, and answer her questions.

"I'm staying–" he started, "I can't remember right now the name of the hotel, but I have it on the tip of my tongue; it'll come back to me in a minute."

"Yeah? Give me a list of things that you did since getting up this morning, then. Did you shave? Did you have breakfast?"

She was hammering questions at him, at a pace with which he was unable to cope. His head was spinning from all the queries. He tried to focus and answer at least one of them, but he wasn't able to visualize the answer. She put a hand on his arm and lowered her voice. Her hand was shaking, and he thought that she was crying, but she had turned her head away from him, and he couldn't be sure.

"Do you remember any of it? Do you?" she asked, almost shouting. "No you don't!" she answered without waiting for his reply, "because you didn't get up this morning."

He looked at her, alarmed by her emotional behavior. She was definitely crying now, but she soon took hold of herself and started talking in a low undertone that was barely audible.

"When you approached me that night," she said without looking at him, "you looked so much like your father that I knew you immediately."

"But you can't know my father. He's been dead for years now, and you hadn't been born when we left the country."

"Please, let me tell this in my own way," she almost begged. "This isn't going to be easy for either of us. This is not the first time that we've met. Do you remember a time when your mother went away for a few weeks, to sit at your grandmother's bedside? You were left alone with your father. Remember?"

He nodded almost imperceptibly. He remembered such a time, but how could she know, he wondered.

"And do you remember a young friend of your father's who would sometimes come and sit beside you, and hold your hand until you fell asleep?"

"How do you know all this?" He had forgotten all about it until now, but she was right. There had been such a young girl and, although he could remember almost nothing about her, he did remember that she had been kind to him when he was afraid to go to sleep all alone. "I never told anybody. My father said that this was to be our little secret, because it was part of a big surprise that he was preparing for Mommy's return, and I was never to tell anybody, otherwise the surprise would be spoiled. And I never did. I am quite sure of it."

"I know it, because I was that girl," she said simply, looking straight in his eyes.

"You must be kidding!" he half laughed, half shouted." I'm much older than you. This is impossible."

She took his hand and spoke in a whisper, "Don't you understand, yet? Can't you see what's happening to you?" His expression showed no comprehension, so she went on, quietly, almost whispering.

"Sometimes, when people die, they don't let go of their previous life. They cling to it, for many different reasons. Some are in denial, and refuse to admit their fate. Others have unfinished business that they must complete before crossing that meadow."

He was shaking his head now, as if to shake away the first drops of understanding, and she went on.

"It's not a happy situation for those of us who cannot cross the meadow yet. We don't belong here. We are intruders, but the living ones usually can't see us. Sometimes they can sense us, and we can manifest ourselves to them, particularly to our loved ones. However, we can never have any real contact with them, and seeing them may be very painful. Some of us are malicious, and spend their time trying to harass the living ones–just as they did when they were alive. But mostly, we are very, very sad, and wish we could reach the point where we can let go of this world."

"But, but–then what I'm doing here? What happened to me? Why?" He was no longer refusing to believe her tale. In fact, he now felt that he had known the truth all along, but had closed his eyes to it.

"You are like the rest of us. For some reason, you can't let go of this world. Some people need help, like that poor child who died in the car crash. And then you come to terms with it, and you let go."

He sat there, in silence, reconciling to what he had known for some time, but had refused to accept. There was no doubt as to the truth of what she had told him. He couldn't remember staying anywhere in town. In fact, since getting here he had roamed the streets or sat at the same old café, looking out of the window. He hadn't slept, shaved, eaten, or performed any other corporeal activity. And he had no idea of how he had gotten here. He definitely had not taken a flight from home.

With this understanding came the chilling realization that he had been haunting his own house. He had been sitting in his living room night after night, at least for a while after his death, content to watch his wife and daughter reading, or watching TV. Just happy to be around them. He felt irrationally frightened for his family.

A thought occurred to him; something that had been on his mind since that evening at the monument. "What did you tell the boy? He was smiling when he went with his nanny."

"That was not his nanny; she was one of the keepers who help those who are undecided. I told him the truth, that his parents too had died in the crash, and that he was going to meet them soon. He was a very strong and mature boy, and he understood."

"But what could be the reason for me being here? I died; I understand that now. I must have died of a heart attack–I had been suffering a little lately–but I sincerely can't remember anything about my death. And there must be a reason for me being damned to stay here."

"Nobody remembers the moments of his death. You find out about it by watching mourning relatives or friends, but you never carry the experience of death with you. The reason why you are here is, I believe, that you have some unfinished business. There is no other reason why you should be standing here, watching this house all the time. And I believe I know what that business is."

"You couldn't know," he said, remembering, too late, the many things she knew about him, "because this has to do with a dream."

And he told her of his nightmare. He had never told the dream to anybody except his wife, and he only did so now with difficulty.

"I knew it!" she said triumphantly, when he finished his tale. "Now let me tell you a story." She stopped, as if to collect her thoughts, and continued. "It was almost thirty-four years ago. I was sitting here, at the very same table were you saw me on the first night, when your father came in. I had been 'doing the life' only for a few weeks, but I already felt like an old lady, although I was only twenty-one years old. We looked at each other for a second, and that was all there was to it. I soon became his mistress. He provided well for me, to make sure that I would not go on working or meeting other men. I think I fell in love with him at once.

"Your mother went away, as I was saying, for a long visit to your grandmother who was ill, and I moved into the house. Then the arguments began. I loved your father, and I wanted to spend the rest of my life with him. I didn't understand then that what he saw in me, was what I was—a whore. Pretty, yes. Innocent in many senses, yes. Still, nothing more than a toy for him.

"Your father, I'm sorry to say, was a very cruel man. He didn't care at all about your mother, but had to put up with her because the money that went into the family business was hers. He didn't care much about you either, although probably he had a greater interest in you than he had in anybody else. The only thing that really counted for him was his social position. He had to marry well, and to have a son who was well behaved by his own standards. He once told me that you would learn to behave yourself even if it killed you, and what's more, you would learn to like it."

Her words were like salt strewn on an open wound to him. During the years, he had tried hard to love his father, but the best he had been able to do was to fear him. He knew that his father was hard, and was not surprised to hear that he was evil too. "One day he called me and told me that your mother was expected back the next week," she continued, "and that I was to clear out. He said that he would continue to see me on a regular basis, but I wasn't to come near the house unless sent for. By then, I was no longer ready to give your father up to anybody, not even to his rightful wife. So I made a scene, and I told him that he had to get a divorce and marry me. I told him that I was pregnant–which was a lie, but he couldn't know–and that I would create a scandal that would ruin him, unless he married me. My recollection of what happened next is a bit blurred, and incoherent, but I am pretty sure that we had a horrible fight.

"Then, one day, I found myself sitting at this table. It took me a while to sort things out, and to understand that I was no longer alive, but with that realization came the determination to find out what had happened to me. I had to know whether I had died of an accident, or of a disease, or whether–an unbearable thought–your father's hand was behind it.

"I started looking around, hoping to hear things. As you have learned by now, we can't influence matter very much. We can manifest ourselves, but we can't move objects, except with the greatest effort, and only in some cases. I didn't know how many days had passed since my death, but certainly there was nothing about it in the daily newspapers, and I couldn't go to a library and look through the old ones. I tried to stay close to your father, in the house and out, hoping to hear something–but nothing. He never breathed a word about me to anybody, never visited my grave, wherever that was, nor did he show any sign of distress at my death. Life in your house went on as usual, until one day you all packed-up, and were gone. And I was left here, to wonder what had happened to me, unable to let go."

"Poor child!" He sympathized with her, knowing well how detached and matter-of-fact his father had been, and how easily this could have broken a young girl's heart. He tried to imagine his father in the role of a murderer. It was not so difficult to believe that he might have killed to avoid a scandal. However, there were many other possible explanations: an accident could have occurred, or she could have killed herself when his father had made it clear to her that under no circumstances would he marry her. There was no telling what might have really happened.

"This must be terrible for you. But you will have to give up. There is no point for you to go on suffering."

"Yes, there is–or rather, there was. I think I know now. Your dream tells all. I think it could have been me you saw being buried under the tub. And the man of your dream must have been your father. You may have caught him in the act, and either you didn't understand what you saw, or your mind just shut it out, except when dreaming."

The thought that she might be right was horrifying. Yet, the possibility was there, making chilling sense.

"Well, I guess we'll never know–and I'm not so sure now that I want to know," he said.

"But you must find out, you have to!" she appealed to him, "That is why you are here. If you stop searching for the truth, you'll be stuck here for ever, with me, asking yourself what really happened, and whether your nightmare was true."

"But what can I do? You yourself said that we can't move things. So many years have passed, and my father is dead. There is nobody else to turn to for help. It's a hopeless situation."

"So you want to get stuck here, looking out of this dirty window for ever? And I should keep walking around restless? I don't think so."

"Well, I don't know what else we can do."

"I do," she said. "I have a plan."

"What plan?" he asked in disbelief.

"I'll tell you. But first, we are taking a little trip," she said, taking his hand and dragging him out.

CHAPTER IV
The Tram

The tram moved along its tortuous path, making grinding noises and, now and then, halting with a jerk. The time was ten thirty p.m. by the clock that stood near the last stop. Clara and George sat on the bench of an almost empty car, looking out as the city unwound before them. A young girl and a middle-aged man, both sitting facing them, were the only other travelers. The girl listened to pop music through headphones that did little to prevent the sound from filling the car. She was perhaps eighteen years old, and wore a T-shirt that didn't cover her belly, and which left no doubt that she was not wearing a bra. Her blue jeans were happily torn throughout, and looked more like a rag than anything else. The middle-aged man glared at her with unconcealed disapproval.

They had boarded the tramcar at a station near his former home. George had stood on the platform near the stop with the number of the line they had planned to take, along with the living people who waited for other trams. While waiting, he had looked with interest at the signs. They had changed since his childhood, and were much more modern and friendly. The sign near which they stood indicated that there was a priority line for senior citizens. Maybe they'd put up signs for ghosts as well, he reflected, if this went on for long.

"I wonder whether there are other dead people here, waiting for the tram. What do you think?" he asked her.

"I doubt it. I like to get around in this way, but I guess that there is little point for most people in our condition. Anyway, it's not so easy to spot them, unless you get close and check if they are seeing you. Even then, you can be mistaken. I've had cases in which I could have sworn that someone was looking at me and seeing me, when it turned out that he just looked at everything in the same idiotic way. After a while, you stop caring. Even if you come across someone you know, it's not much of a conversation. Everybody seems to be pretty much taken up with their own problems, and nobody seems to like to chat for the fun of it. You are the first one with whom I actually enjoy talking."

They stood on the platform for a while, and when the car arrived they hopped on. As they slid past the conductor George felt a pang of guilt; it was the first time he had ever taken a ride without paying the fare. They sat in the car, and he gazed at the middle-aged man and at the girl, still amazed at the thought that they were not seeing him, and realizing that he still needed some time to adjust to his new condition.

"You know," he said, "I don't 'feel' dead. It feels the same as always, only a little strange."

"It takes a while to get used to it. At first, I couldn't believe that people weren't seeing me. I would make faces at them, and talk to them, and, of course, nothing happened. They really didn't see me. One day, I decided to see what happens if you 'collide' with a living person. I was on a tram just like this, and there was a man heading for an empty seat. I raced him and sat in his place. He went on and sat on me, as if I weren't there."

"And what happened?"

"Nothing much. It felt uncomfortable, almost unclean, to sit there, blending with a living person. So, I just moved aside, and that was it. He never felt a thing–or if he did, I didn't notice."

George fell into a thoughtful silence. The lights outside the tram window illuminated scenes of his youth. That small ice-cream place was where he and his friends used to meet often on Saturday evenings, to talk aloud about girls and other things they didn't understand, and to pass the time.

Now, he found himself reflecting, he would never taste ice cream again. He didn't feel the urge, though. He wondered whether this was what death is about, not wanting anything anymore. If this is all there is to death, then this earth was full of half-living, half-dead people, who did not want any real thing, and only thought that what they want will provide happiness. He considered that he might be more alive now than his insurance broker had ever been, although he was still breathing and infesting the street of his hometown.

"Okay, now," Clara said, "let's get down to work. I brought you here for a purpose. I want to show you what we can do with living persons."

"I thought you said that there is nothing we can do."

"Well, we can't actually *do* anything to them. But we can make *them* do things."

"I don't follow you. Either we can, or we can't do things."

"Listen, here is the thing. We can influence a living person to act as we wish, by putting ideas into his head. But you can't accomplish very much in this way. You can't make them do something that is against their will, unless they are not thinking about it. If they resist, there is nothing we can do."

"And how do we make them do what we want?"

"We just think about it. We think that we want them to do something, like scratching their head, or crossing their legs, and they do it."

"And how, pray, is our ability to make them scratch their heads going to do us any good? I thought you had an idea. If your idea is to go around in trams, making perfect strangers scratch their heads, you can count me out."

"If you can stop being a sarcastic ass for a moment, I'll tell you. We can't move things–or at least, not often and not much–but we may cause living people to do it. And we can create noises, and make people believe they are seeing things–at least if they are receptive enough. If we can put the idea into the heads of the people who live in your house that the tub must be replaced or fixed, they'll do it, and we will be there to see. This is how we find out if there is anything real in your dream."

"And how are we going to do that?"

"We can cause small problems, such a leaks and noises, which can be attributed to the water system. That house is very old, as you know. It was old when you left it, and the new owners have done nothing to improve it. The whole building is in bad shape. If they think that there is a problem with the system, they will have to do something about it."

"Well, if this is your idea—and I'm not telling you that I like it—then what are we doing here?"

"I need to teach you how to exercise your powers, and the tram is the best place to start. Here people stay put for the duration of the ride, and usually have nothing to do, so we can learn how to influence them. Look what I'm going to do with that man over there."

The man had sat quietly since coming on board, and had started to doze off. Now, he extended his forefinger, touched the side of his nose, and then touched the sole of his left shoe.

"You see?" she asked with girlish satisfaction, "I made him do it."

"You made him do what?"

"I made him touch his nose and the sole of his shoe."

"Well, I am impressed!"

"Stop sneering, you idiot! That was just a demonstration."

"I'm sorry. I keep forgetting that it's not your fault I'm here, and that I should not be taking it out on you. But really, now, how do you know that he didn't do that of his own free will? Maybe your power is not to make him *do* things, but rather to anticipate what he is going to do?"

"Okay, I'll prove it to you. Tell me what you want him to do."

"Let him get up, go to the end of the car, flex his knees and go back to sit down."

"We are demanding, aren't we? Well, I'll try."

The middle-aged man had dozed off again, and he now stirred and got up. He walked to the end of the car, as if to renew his blood circulation, shook his leg and went back to his seat.

"Well, that didn't really count as flexing his legs, but you made your point. Now let me try. Do you think I can make that girl take off her headphones and offer them to her fellow traveler?"

"You can try. He is not going to like it, though."

"Who cares? Watch me!"

He concentrated on the girl, imagining her movements as she performed the acts he had planned for her. She took the headphones off, and he felt inebriated. She offered them to the middle-aged man, who frigidly refused, and he felt elated. He was not entirely estranged from this world then, he thought. There was still a thread that connected him to it. He still belonged!

"Very good!" she applauded. "It took me a long time to be able to do things like that. But then, of course, I didn't have a great mentor to teach me..."

The middle-aged man was now taking off his shoes and putting them neatly beside him on the seat. He then gawked at them, as if seeing them for the first time, blushed, and put them on again without looking in the direction of the girl sitting beside him.

"You shouldn't have done that!" she cried. "You are not supposed to use this power to cause embarrassment."

"I'm sorry, but I couldn't help it. I had to teach him a lesson. He is such a pompous ass that he deserved it."

"Well, don't do it again. We must start being constructive. We must plan what to do."

"You keep saying that. But why must we? The only privilege of being dead is that we must do nothing. And nothing we do has any meaning or real effect anyway. So why bother?

And what's the rush?"

"You think you have time, don't you?" Clara said angrily. "I've been here for thirty-three years, with no end in sight, damned to walk these streets in the hope of finding a random clue to my death. Now you come, as a God-sent link to that time, to raise my hopes that maybe I can find out what happened and be free. This is no joke for me. And you'll find out that it's no joke for you too, if you stick around long enough."

A tear had appeared in the corner of her eyes, and it made him panic. The one thing he had never learnt to cope with was a girl crying. His daughter, George remembered, had learnt of his weakness in the cradle, had always used it lavishly and it never failed to get her what she wanted.

He took her hand and squeezed hard.

"You are crying! I didn't know dead people could cry. Don't do it, please."

"I can't help it. I haven't spoken to anybody more than a few words since—since that day. You're the first, and I have nobody else to turn to for help. Everybody else is too busy with their own problems."

"I'll help. You know I will. I am your friend, and I'll do what I can. Only, you know, I'm having a hard time myself figuring all this out. Nevertheless, you and I are in this together, and we will help each other. Besides," he said with a smile, "I still owe you for those evenings when I was scared stiff and you held my hand and sung me to sleep."

"You were such a cute boy, polite and friendly," she said. "Nothing like now," she added with fake severity. "I used to sit beside you and dream that you, your father and I would be a happy family forever after. I think I really liked you then."

"You do keep saying 'then', don't you?" She was her composed self again, and he was determined to keep her busy talking. "By the way, how come that you feel real to me, and I can touch you and feel the pressure of your hand?"

"I don't know, but it's not the same with everybody. Some of us have no consistency at all, and others feel real like you and me. It may have to do with the stage we are in, but I don't know. I'm glad," she added as an afterthought, "that we can feel each other. It makes us closer, I think."

"I guess you're right. But I am fed up with this tram and that music. Why don't we get off and go to work?"

"Do you think that you are up to it already?" she asked wistfully.

"Watch me. For me to think and to act are but one. I will be canceling all my other appointments for you," he laughed. "I won't be outdone in politeness by that ugly child I used to be."

"You lead!" Clara said. She was definitely smiling now.

George smiled back to her, pleased that he had, at least, accomplished this much.

He gazed out of the window at the approaching station, hoping that the tram would slow down and stop. He looked forward to getting busy with anything that would make Clara feel better.

A handful of people stood waiting at the stop, and the tram came to a halt near them. Clara and George stepped down and started walking away from the car. A man was standing near the stop sign. George recognized him immediately. Clara had seen him too, and stood a few steps behind, while George walked up to him.

"Uncle Henry, I presume," he said.

"So it's really you, George?" said the man.

"It's me, Uncle. How are you?"

"Well, that's a hell of a question, you know. You have grown up quite a bit," he said, sounding amazed. "I spotted you before, but I wasn't sure that it was really you. I haven't seen you since you were little, but you resemble your father." He stopped for a moment, assuming a dreamy expression, then continued. "And you have your mother's eyes. Yes, I should have known right away that it was you."

"But why didn't you approach me when you saw me?"

"I wasn't sure. We—you know, we tend to be a little shy, and we respect each other's privacy. But now, come here and give me a hug."

George was embarrassed, but hugging his uncle was good. It felt like family. Clara had been standing aside, trying not to intrude. She was excluded from this reunion, and he felt guilty for it.

"George, my boy," said his uncle, "we have a lot of threads to pick up, but not here. Come with me where we can talk quietly."

George eyed Clara who, as if guessing his thoughts, approached them.

"George," she said, "don't let me detain you. I am sure that you and your uncle have a lot to talk about. Why don't you go with him? We can continue with our plans when you two have had the time to get reacquainted."

"You wouldn't mind that?" George asked, gratefully.

"Of course not. Don't be silly. I'll be waiting for you. When you are ready, you'll find me at the café."

She turned around and started to walk away.

"Hey!" George called. Approaching her as she stopped, he took her hand in his and squeezed it. "Thanks for being so understanding," he said. "All this is still a bit bewildering to me, and maybe talking to Uncle will do me good."

"No problem," she said, "I'll be waiting for you."

George turned back to his uncle and looked at him again. He was still very much as he remembered him—short and stocky, and with thinned out gray hair. But he was his only uncle, and a beloved link to his past.

"Where are we going, Uncle?" he asked.

"I'll take you home, my boy," he said simply.

CHAPTER V
Uncle Henry

"A hell of a dream, you've been having, my boy," said Uncle Henry, when George finished telling him of his trouble. "What did your parents say about it?"

"Well, I had that dream for the first time about ten months before we left for the USA. I remember as if it were yesterday how I woke up in terror in my room. I didn't know if I was still dreaming or not. Mother was away and I went to my father's room and climbed into bed with him."

"That took some guts," said Uncle Henry. "Your father couldn't have liked it."

"No, he didn't. You know how he hated physical contact. But for once I was more scared of the nightmare than of him. And you should have heard how he yelled at me. He told me that people would think that I was insane, to dream insane dreams like this. He ordered me never to tell anybody about it.

He made me promise that I would not disgrace myself and my parents by making a fool of myself in public."

"I know, I know. Your father had always been too conscious of what strangers might think of him. I could never understand why appearances were so important to him. So what happened next?"

"Well, I had no choice but to promise that I would never tell anybody about my dream. I resolved to forget all about it, but the nightmare came again, only a few days later. This time both my parents rushed to my room. I wanted to tell mother about my dream, but one look at my father was enough stop me."

"So what did you do?"

"I told them that I dreamt that there were little green monsters in my room." He remembered how lights had been turned on, and beds looked under, until he had finally gotten under the sheets again, feeling awful about having lied to his mother.

"And you never told your mother?"

"No. Mother was always ready to comfort and console. When she was around, that is. But she was often away from home for long spells, at Granny's bedside–and when she was home, you know how dreamy she was."

"She lived in a world of her own, didn't she? But that was part of her charm."

"Yes," George said fondly, "she was vague at times, but always caring and gentle."

"How did she do during the last years?"

"She was very happy," George lied quickly. What was the point of saddening his uncle? The truth was that she had been thoroughly unhappy. She had died first, a few years ago, and he had watched his father through the difficult days of the preparations for the funeral and the ceremony, hoping to see signs of grief at the loss. He had not seen any. And he had hated him for it, and he still hated him when, two years later, his father had died suddenly. He had tried hard to grieve then, but his eyes had remained dry.

"I miss her very much, you know," Uncle Henry said. "I hoped to see her around, but she hasn't come. I hope she remembers her brother."

"I'm sure she does, Uncle. She always was very fond of you."

"I always wondered whether you married. Tell me a little about your family."

"My wife, Jane, is a quiet, caring person, very devoted to me and to our daughter, Sharon. She reminds me in many ways of Mother. You would have liked her. Although they do have a tendency, between the two of them, to be a bit bossy."

He remembered a night when he had come home to find that the sitting room had been redecorated. The chairs and tables had been shifted around so that no two persons could sit comfortably, and at the same time have a conversation; new curtains (of a color scheme that he particularly disliked) hung at the windows, and a new carpet had taken the place of the old, battered rug he liked so much.

"What do you think, honey?" his wife had asked.

He had looked at her expectant face, clearly waiting for his praise, and had shifted his gaze to his daughter's, which clearly said "I dare you say something bad about it!"

So he had taken control of his drooping face, and had said,

"Why, it's nice."

"Only nice?" his wife had prompted him.

"Well, I wish you'd left the old carpet in place. It was cozy."

"Nonsense! It was torn up to pieces. It had to go."

"But, do you think that we could move that armchair there a little closer to the window?"

"Oh! I don't know. We have been working so hard to plan all this for you, that I really don't think it can be improved upon."

"So, how do you like it, Dad?" his daughter had asked, meaningfully.

"It's nice," he had forced himself to say. "Quite nice, yes." There the matter had rested. He had often wondered whether that evening symbolized the essence of his relationship with the women of his life.

George was absorbed in conversation and had paid little attention to the streets in which they were walking, but now they had reached a part of town that was familiar to him. They stopped outside the bar where, in hot summer days, he had used to go to quench his thirst after roaming the streets on his bicycle. The bar hadn't changed a bit. It was still dark and full of glass that reflected whatever little light the owner was willing to allow his customers to enjoy.

"Would you mind waiting for a minute?" George asked. "I'd like to go inside and take a look. I haven't seen this place in years."

"Go ahead, my boy. Take your time. Meanwhile I'll be strolling here in front."

George stepped in. The bar was L-shaped, and drinking glasses hung upside-down from an L-shaped ledge. At the long end a young bartender was wiping the glasses with a towel. He worked methodically, taking one glass at a time from the ledge, wiping it, and replacing it onto the ledge. He looked bored, and was probably killing time between customers. Every now and then he would stop, put down the rug on the counter, and turn to look at himself in the mirror behind. Apparently unsatisfied with his looks, he would re-arrange his hair with his fingers, and then get back to work.

At the short end of the bar he spotted a second bartender. This one was approximately his age, and looked familiar. He couldn't remember his name, but he was sure now; he had been at school with him. And a lousy scholar he had been, always busy brawling with the boys and never paying any attention to the lessons.

This bartender was eyeing his younger colleague with malevolence, and was taking down from the ledge above him glasses that looked freshly wiped, wiping them all over again and putting them back in the same place. He looked at him in amazement, as he finished wiping the entire row of glasses, and then started wiping them all over again. He lifted his head for a moment and gave George a quick, uninterested gaze.

George walked up to him with a friendly smile.

"Hello. Remember me?" he said.

The bartender looked up, stopping his wiping for a second, lowered his eyes again and went on with his work.

"Yeah, I guess I do," he said quietly. "You were that malicious kid sitting just before me, who would never throw me a bone during the tests. God, did I hate you then! You were so polite, so well behaved, and so respectful to the teacher, that you made me want to throw up. I hope you have improved over the years. What are you doing here?"

He was taken aback by the swift, full, and precise disclosure of his "defects," as seen through the eyes of a boy.

"I gotta hand it to you—you do have a memory." He avoided the question regarding his reasons for being here. He certainly would not bare his soul to this erstwhile childhood schoolmate, after a gap of so many years. "But tell me. Why do you take up those glasses, which have been thoroughly wiped, and wipe them again? And they are not *real* glasses anyway, right? Living persons can't see them."

The bartender's look of shock, close to terror, told him that he must have asked the wrong question. He opened his mouth, then closed it, then opened it again, starting to talk fast and loud.

"Why do I wipe them? Why, you ask? *Because!* Yes, sir, this is my job," he was shouting by now, "it's my job to see to it that the glasses are clean. What kind of bartender would I be, if I let my customers drink out of unwiped glasses? Some nerve, you have, coming in and asking me such a question. Isn't it enough that you didn't help me on the final math test? And then you have to come in and criticize!"

He lowered his voice, as if suddenly aware of its extreme loudness, and continued, in a reproachful tone.

"You know, I could have been somebody today, had I not failed the math test. And what happened when I failed, you may ask? My father sent me to work in my uncle's shop. To learn to be a butcher. That's what happened. All day in a smelly shop, going in and out of a freezer, carrying raw meat. Every other week I would get home with a cold on account of that freezer. I never got used to cutting through flesh and bones. This is why I'm not a butcher today. Do you get it?"

Throughout the bartender's outburst George had stood petrified. He could barely remember this person, and couldn't recall his name at all. Yet, he was just learning that he–not anybody else–had been the reason for the failure of this man's life. The bartender went on.

"It all happened so quickly. After I failed the test, my father said that he was through wasting good money on a nitwit like me. I was to earn my living he said, and to learn that you don't waste good opportunities that your loving parents and Good Providence put your way. So, since I hadn't made the little effort to study mathematics, I was going to pay now. And you know the worst of it? I did study. I studied hard, and I knew some of it. Not enough to pass the test, though. But I'm convinced that I would have pulled through, if only a good soul had helped me pass that one test."

"I–I had no idea. I can't tell you how sorry I am. But I really don't recall refusing to help you."

"Oh, yes. Yes, yes, yes, yes! That is just like you! I wasn't important enough to you, was I, you self-centered little spoiled brat. I bet you didn't even notice when I left school, I was that unimportant to you."

And, in fact, George realized that he hadn't noticed. Up to now he had never taken the time to wonder what had happened to his classmate, after that year's exams period.

He felt ashamed now, and his only wish was to get away as quickly as possible from this raging bartender. He muttered a few unintelligible words of belated apology, turned on his heels and walked out, accompanied by the chant of the never-ending list of his sins.

His uncle was outside, sitting on an ancient brick wall and

looking at two children playing an elaborate catching game. Suddenly he felt sad, remembering that he had been a child just like them, right here, not a long time ago. He realized that there were no happy memories–at least, not around here.

"Can we keep going?" his uncle asked.

"Yes, Uncle. Let's go," he said, looking over his shoulder. The bartender was nowhere in sight, he noted with relief.

CHAPTER VI
The League

George and Uncle Henry had been walking through an old, desolate neighborhood. Many buildings seemed to be barely inhabited, and only few lights filtered through their windows. They now reached a decrepit red brick building and entered its garden through a corroded iron gate. X-shaped wooden bars, nailed into the fixtures, blocked the ground floor windows. A sign put up by the City Engineer's Office read, "Danger! Condemned Building. Keep Out!".

"Here we are," said Uncle Henry, "this is where I live. Let's hurry. I want to make it to the tenants' meeting."

Before George was able to ask what "a tenants' meeting" was, Uncle Henry led him into a large room on the ground floor, which was badly lit by the street lamps outside its windows. In the room, a small crowd of about forty people was scattered around, mostly standing, and some sitting on an occasional chair. A dignified lady of middle age was having an argument with a gentleman of military appearance, who sat at a table together with a fat matron and a young woman. The matron didn't speak, but scanned the room with piercing eyes. The younger woman reminded George of his dentist's secretary, and looked similarly bored. The gentleman who sat with them, on the contrary, seemed to be taking something very much to heart.

"We can't have that there here," he was saying emphatically. "This is very damaging to our condominium. Very bad for the image. Bad for the image, very bad." He sat down, then got up again and added, as in an afterthought, "This depreciates our property. It's unacceptable. Insufferable. Can't have that. It..." He paused for a moment, as if to find the punch line, then his face lit up. "Our property gets depreciated," he said and, having apparently shot his bolt, he sat down.

"But, Colonel," said the lady in the crowd, speaking with admirable patience, "where can my boys play, if not on the grass in front of the building? What harm do they do? I know they may be a little noisy at times, but they mean no harm."

"They mean no harm?" repeated the colonel, rising indignantly. "So that's what they mean? No harm? They spend their time making a racket under my window. That's what they do. No harm, you say, bah!"

"I understand that they shouted under your window yesterday," said the lady. "They are sorry for it, but boys will be boys."

"Not while I am on this committee, they won't," said the colonel, rising again. "If my esteemed colleagues, the lady members of the committee, agree, I would propose taking a vote." He looked inquiringly at the fat matron, who nodded curtly.

The one that George had labeled "the secretary," said, "All right, Colonel. No need to get worked up about it. We can have a vote, if you insist."

"I insist. I insist," said the Colonel.

"All those in favor of prohibiting children's play on the grounds of our building, please raise your hands," said the secretary.

Three or four hands were raised.

"Thank you," she said, ignoring the colonel who was beaming at them with gratification. "Those against the motion, please raise your hands now."

About fifteen hands were raised.

"Okay. Let's take a count. Ten, eleven. Motion not adopted."

The fat matron spoke for the first time. "Thanks everybody. Meeting adjourned."

The crowd was now dispersing. George, who throughout the exchanges between the lady and the Colonel had been trying to understand what was going on, turned to Uncle Henry.

"Uncle, can you explain what this was all about?" he asked.

"Yes, of course. This was a meeting held to discuss various problems that bother the tenants of this building. We pride ourselves of being civilized and able to resolve any differences in a democratic manner. You won't find any feuds among the people who live in this building. We air all our differences and we solve them before they get out of hand. What you just witnessed was a discussion on the last item on the agenda. This is the old argument about Mrs. Rothstein's children. Mrs. Rothstein is a Viennese–she is that lady over there," he said, pointing at the woman that had been arguing with the colonel at the meeting, who was shepherding two children that kept close to her black skirt, "and her two children are a plague. They keep playing around the building at all hours, and some of the people here are quite vexed with them."

"But, I don't understand," said George, perplexed. "This is an old building that looks like it's going to fall apart soon. Are all these people haunting it?"

"We don't like the verb 'haunt', at all. We very much prefer 'inhabit'," Uncle Henry said severely, "but wait a second, I want to have a word with the colonel."

The colonel had finished what seemed to be a heated argument with one of the people at the other end of the room, and was now walking toward the door, where George and Uncle Henry were standing.

"Colonel," said Uncle Henry. "Allow me to congratulate you. A very good speech. Indeed, the best you have given, to date, on the subject."

"Thank you, Henry. I'm flattered," he winked, "although I thought it pretty good myself. And who," he asked, eyeing George, "do we have here?"

"Allow me to introduce my nephew, George. He is new and has just joined us."

"Hello, George," said the colonel. "Welcome, welcome. We need young blood. Young blood. That's what we need, indeed. Welcome. Well," he added, "I must move on. I'll be seeing you around."

"He doesn't look sad at all," George wondered aloud, after the Colonel had left them, "in spite of the fact that he was voted down right now."

"Oh, that...he didn't really expect the vote to pass. It never does. In fact, nobody really wants it to pass, seeing that it's such a nice item to have on the agenda of the tenants' meetings. That's why the motion is never accepted."

"But—how often do you have these meetings?"

"Why, every day, of course. They never stop. This is the job of the people on the Tenants' Committee. I used to be on the committee too, for a while, but then I got bored with it. My current job is much better."

"Job?" George was confused. Was his uncle really dead? Were all these people dead, or not? And if they were, what was his uncle talking about?

"Yes. Now I am a lighting inspector. I cover the city center, and if a lamppost is out of order, I report it to the Lighting Committee. In this way we contribute to the life of the city."

"And what does the Lighting Committee *do* with your report?"

"Of course, it does its best to bring the problem to the attention of City Hall, with a view to having it corrected. You can't imagine how many problems would go unnoticed if it weren't for us."

"But, Uncle," George continued, feeling dizzy, "what's all this in aid of? Why the meetings? Why worry about this old building that is going to fall apart anyway? And what was all that burbling about the value of the property? What property? In short, Uncle," asked George, growing excited by his own questions, "what on earth are you all talking about?"

"My boy," said Uncle Henry, patiently, "I can see that you are a little confused. And who wouldn't be? You are new to all this, and I haven't even explained about the League, yet."

"League? What League?"

"The League of Continued Life. All the people that you see here are members of the League, as I hope you'll soon be. It's not always easy to be accepted—we must guard ourselves against certain people—but I'm sure that, being my nephew, you'll become a member quite easily. Let's take a seat over here," he said, steering George to a corner of the room, "and I'll tell you all about it.

"Yes," said George, feeling dizzier, "why don't you?"

"The League," Uncle Henry continued, "was founded by Big Maggie—the fat lady that you saw sitting on the committee. Being our founder and spiritual leader, she sits, by right, on all committees. Big Maggie was a spiritualist and a medium in her former life, and she explored the meaning of the afterlife before joining us over here. She was the first to understand that passing away doesn't mean becoming a non-entity, and that life continues after death. She has organized us and has given us the strength to get back to normal, to rationalize our time and to keep our dignity, instead of loafing about as many other dead people do. We owe it to her that this wonderful organization exists, where everyone can still make himself useful, and play a role in the universal scheme of things.

"Before I met Big Maggie, I was a poor soul, walking around aimlessly and feeling useless. I talked to nobody, and nobody talked to me. I was bitter and angry, and I'm sure that I was a most unpleasant person. Now, I have a purpose and something to look forward to. I have friends and acquaintances, as you have seen. Come, I want to introduce you to her."

The room was now almost empty, and Uncle Henry walked George toward a staircase that led to an upper floor. They walked past a door at the top of the stairs, finding themselves in a room that would have been empty but for an old and battered chest of drawers, a chair, and a Queen size bed covered with a red rag. The fat lady from the committee was lying on the bed.

"I hope I'm not disturbing you, Maggie," said Uncle Henry. "I would like you to meet my nephew, George. He has just arrived."

The fat lady sat on the bed and inspected them with porcine eyes.

"Not at all. Pleased to meet you," Maggie said, putting out her hand. George took it and shook it, somewhat surprised by the act that, for some reason, seemed unnatural to him now. "In fact, I was rather expecting you, George."

"You were?" asked George. It was uncanny, since until that moment he didn't even know she existed.

"Yes, I was. There is little I don't know, George. For instance, I know that you lived and died in France."

"America, actually," he corrected her.

"America or France, it doesn't matter," she said, dismissing the issue. "It's abroad, anyway. And, of course, you are a tormented soul who feels you have been wronged in life. I'm sure that right now you would like to take revenge on your enemies."

"Well, you know, I don't actually think that I have any enemies. I'm certainly tormented, though, by my pathetic situation."

"Of course, I knew that," she said with a satisfied smirk. "You should excuse me for sitting on the bed like this, but this is where I pass most of my time. This was my bedroom in my previous life, you know, and I naturally feel comfortable in it."

She got up and walked to the window, looking out, seemingly in deep thought.

"Isn't she something?" whispered Uncle Henry proudly. "Very few elected people get to live in their original house after they pass away. That shows you how privileged she is."

Maggie, having apparently finished her meditation, turned back to them.

"Has Henry already told you about our organization?" she asked.

"I told him the bare essentials," Uncle Henry intervened, "but I'm sure that he has many other questions."

"I'll be pleased to explain everything to him. Would you like me to explain?" she asked, turning to George.

"Yes, please. I could use some explaining, right now."

"Well, it all began many years ago, when I was still alive. I had been blessed with a great gift, the ability to speak with the dead. I devoted my life to helping dead people to contact their relatives and assisted them best as I could. In this way, I was able to learn a lot about what happens after you die, from the experience of the many souls with whom I'd been in touch over the years.

"I finally understood that salvation awaits around the corner, and that we must bring it about by our own acts." She now stood up and opened her hands, with outstretched arms, in an impressive and mystic gesture. George was watching and listening intently.

"We, the members of the League, believe that once the fabric of society has been restored by reoccupying our rightful positions in this world, the day of resurrection will come. On that day we will resume our position in the universe, and all evil will be undone. And we know that the day is almost here," she was now talking loudly and forcefully, and her strength was impossible to resist. George's eyes were riveted to her face. "Now that many of our members are spreading out, reaching for the world, we must intensify our efforts and avoid making mistakes. Welcome to the League, George," she thundered. "I can sense that you are ready to become a member."

George had been adsorbed by the compelling speech that Maggie had just delivered, but a doubt refused to leave his mind.

"But..." he said hesitantly, "what about the meadow? I understand that we must cross the meadow as soon as possible, in order to find peace."

"The meadow," she said, with an exclamation of disgust. "Who's been feeding lies to you? The meadow is a scam. It's a plan of the living people to get rid of us. Do you know what happens when you cross the meadow? No, of course you don't," she added quickly, "or you wouldn't be asking me stupid questions. You cease to exist; that's what happens. That's it. No more George, thank you. And some more room for the living people, once the day of resurrection comes." She now looked angry, and formidable. "This is something that has been invented by the forces of evil in order to shake our faith in the continuity of Life. Those who have doubts can never become members of the League, and they're damned to cross the meadow and be annihilated." Her face was now contorted in an expression of sheer hatred. "If you wish to remain a member of the League, don't you ever mention the meadow to me again," she added. "Understood?"

George nodded in silent assent. He wasn't sure he was getting everything right. But then, he knew, he needed some time to get adjusted to the new world into which he had been plunged. And he was reassured in the knowledge that he could trust his Uncle Henry to guide him and advise him for the best.

"Okay, Henry," Maggie eventually said, her calm self again. "Do you want to go ahead with the initiation ceremony?"

"Yes. I think that the sooner would be the better."

"Let's assemble the Initiation Committee, then," she said.

"Were you calling, Maggie?" The words came from a head that had just popped in through the door. The head was followed by a very short old woman, almost a midget, with an impish smile that contrasted with her wrinkled face.

"No, Agatha," said Maggie, "but we were planning to. We need to assemble the Initiation Committee. Where is James?"

"Who knows," said Agatha with a shrug, "I haven't seen him for days."

Maggie looked annoyed. "It's just like him, never being around when we need him. I don't know why I was too kind-hearted and made him a member of the committee."

"But you remember that the regulations of the Initiation Committee allow us to make anybody a member *ad hoc*, to perform initiations."

"No," said Maggie. "We proposed the rule but never approved it."

"Yes, we did."

"No, we didn't"

"We did, too."

"Ladies," intervened Uncle Henry. "Why don't you vote now? I seem to remember that a committee member and the chairperson are a quorum."

"Quite right," said Agatha. "All in favor raise your hands.

Motion approved," she said, without looking around. "Now, Henry, would you agree to become a temporary member of our committee? Very good," she said when Uncle Henry nodded his consent. "Now, let's all hold hands and concentrate. What's your name?" she asked, turning to George.

"It's George."

"George, you are now formally a member of the League of Continued Life. Congratulations," said Agatha.

"Is that all?" George asked, puzzled.

"Yes, of course. What else do you want?" asked Agatha, giving him a perplexed look. "Well, it was nice meeting you. I gotta go. Much to do. Always busy, always running. But, I mustn't complain," she said, and left the room.

"Thanks, Maggie," said Uncle Henry. "I'll take George for a tour now, to meet some people."

"See you soon, George," said Maggie. "Now it's time for you to decide on a new job. Choose well and you shall be rewarded," she added with a friendly smile. "But if your choice doesn't come from your heart," she added with a frightening scowl, "I'll know it. Believe me, I'll know."

CHAPTER VII
The Museum

George smiled benevolently at the children as they started the tour of the Egyptian exhibition. This was the exhibition he liked most. His colleague was embarking on a long explanation of the dynasty of the kings of ancient Egypt–a speech that George knew by heart by now. He was a very good guide–an Asian, probably a Korean. His nametag read simply "Kim." Kim had been working at the museum for almost ten years now, and knew every corner of the huge building. At first, George was not sure about this job that seemed to require a knowledge that he didn't possess, and doubted he would be able to acquire. But after a few days during which he had followed Kim closely through his tours, he had overcome his diffidence, discovering that he was learning his way around quickly. It was a pity, though, that he had no way to converse with Kim and to ask him questions on exhibits that he never mentioned. He kept very close to him, memorizing his every word, but Kim's explanations were often superficial, only touching on special items when one of the visitors asked a question. George spent much time eavesdropping on visitors who discussed exhibits that were never explained during the tour, trying to satiate his never-ending curiosity.

The idea to apply for the position at the museum had been Agatha's. She had taken an interest in George's future after their first brief meeting in Maggie's room, and was always engaging him in conversation, inquiring about his plans and offering suggestions of all kinds. George had grown fond of this mercurial woman, and enjoyed her company.

"What about a job as a Stop-Light Engineer at Central Station?" she had asked.

"What does a 'Stop-Light Engineer' do?"

"Would you be surprised," she asked back, "if I told you that he looks after the stop lights?"

"Are we trying to break the record for the longest conversation made all of questions without any answers?" George said, smiling.

"Dear George," Agatha said with a sigh, "I sometimes think that there are altogether too many more questions than answers. In any case, you should make up your mind and choose a job. You've been here long enough. Here, listen to this," she said, suddenly brightening up. "I think that there is a vacant position for a guide at the Municipal Museum. How about that?"

"Mmm," mused George, "I've never been very partial to modern art and stuff like that. I find it pretty boring, and I can't bring myself to be enthusiastic about a few pieces of junk glued together that look like nothing on earth."

"It's not that kind of museum. The Municipal Museum hosts exhibits on natural history, science, and archeology. There is much to be learned there."

"And what happens if I don't like it after a while?"

"All you have to do is apply to the Employment Committee for a new position. The Committee must approve your choice of work every time, anyway."

"I didn't know that we had an 'Employment Committee'. Why should anybody care about what I chose to do? It's not as if they were paying me for it."

"Well, imagine that everybody wanted to be a guide at the museum. All other positions would be left vacant, and the museum would be overcrowded. The Employment Committee has the responsibility for achieving an even distribution of jobs. Come, let's go and talk to them."

The Employment Committee had voiced no objection to George's chosen position, and he had decided to start early the next day. His work had started on the wrong foot, however, and he had almost resolved to leave the museum after his first day. He hadn't been at his new job for more than a couple of hours, trying to figure out what his duties might be, when a fat woman approached him. She was accompanied by a girl perhaps twelve years old, who never spoke.

"Good morning," said the woman. "Are you the guide?"

"Yes, ma'am," George replied, eager to please, "I'm the new guide."

"Isabelle here," she said, pointing at the girl, "would like to make the tour of the Sacred Cats artifacts, particularly those brought from the Valley of the Kings."

The girl avoided looking at him and didn't say a word, as if to dissociate herself entirely from the proceedings. The woman, conversely, gazed at him intently, as if to gauge whether he had been properly impressed by her specific and knowledgeable request.

"I am sorry, ma'am, but I'm new here and I'm not yet familiar with that exhibition. Perhaps you would care to come back some other day?"

"Where is the other guide? The regular guy, I mean?" She did nothing to conceal her annoyance.

"I couldn't say," said George. "There was nobody here when I started today, and I wasn't told that there was somebody else in this position. I rather think that there is nobody else here. You will have to be patient."

"Patience is always invoked by incompetence," the woman said ungraciously. "If you are not qualified, why do you waste other people's time? How is my Isabelle going to learn now? We will have to leave and come back again when they provide a decent guide."

"You do as you please," George was disconcerted by her behavior, but had no intention to engage in a brawl with this distasteful woman. "What I can suggest, for the time being, is that you follow the tour guided by the living guide, Kim. It has just started and I'm sure that you'll get a lot of interesting information from him."

"Are you suggesting that my Isabelle and I should attach ourselves to a crowd of common children? Guess again, then. We are leaving. This is most irregular. I will report you to the Complaints Committee. And I plan to be very strong about it. I am not used to half measures."

"I'm sure you know the way out," said George, losing his

patience and turning his back to them. The need to serve other people had never before come up in his life, nor had he been obliged to take abuse from the customers. If this was what his job was going to look like, he reflected that perhaps he was better off without work. This had been a very bad first day at work for him. He hoped that better ones were in store for him in the future.

Time had gone by and George had become absorbed in his new job. He had learned a lot and had grown to enjoy the task of guiding visitors through the many exhibits in the museum. His only regret was that the calls for his services were few and far between, and he would remain idle for days in a row. Still, he thought with something nearing pride, he was always there, available for every visitor.

"George–"

The voice was a familiar one. George turned to face Clara. He felt embarrassed. He had completely forgotten about her, their meeting and their plans, so much he had been kept busy by his new social circle and the planning of his continued life.

"Well," she said, "this is a bit thick. I take my eyes off you for a second, and look what happens. Do you realize that you've kept me waiting in that café for months? I didn't know what to think. At one point I even thought that, maybe, you had crossed the meadow after all, and here I was, stuck in this city all alone again. And all the while you were having fun here. What do you have to say for yourself?"

"I–I'm sorry. This was quite inconsiderate of me. I should've let you know where I was staying, but the truth is–"

"Staying? What do you mean staying? You're not staying anywhere. Dead people don't 'stay', remember?"

"Well, we of the League beg to differ," George recited from one of Maggie's speeches. "We don't feel that we are second-rate persons only because we happen to have passed away. We feel good about our being, and ourselves, and we live constructive and useful lives. For myself, I'm staying with my uncle in a very nice and well-organized residence."

"The League!" she exclaimed, almost in anguish. "Do you mean to tell me that you've become involved with those nuts?"

"I don't know why you should be calling us nuts. That's not very nice of you."

"Is it already 'us', then?" she asked, eyeing him narrowly.

"Yes. I went through the initiation ceremony on the same day that we met my uncle, and I became a full member of the League. Maybe you could become a member too."

"Not while I have all my screws on. Do you believe all that crap about the resurrection?"

"Well, I can't say that I'm certain about it all, but it makes some sense, and I don't really mind, as long as my daily life is pleasant and comfortable. I live with Uncle Henry, you know, and it's nice not to be alone."

"Yeah," she said bitterly, "for a while after I met you I also thought that I wasn't alone anymore. But now I see that I was wrong."

"It doesn't have to be that way," George said, pleadingly. "You can come with me and become a member too. Even if you're not a great believer in Continued Life, it doesn't matter. What matters is that you can live in our community and not be alone. All you have to do is to pay lip service to the purposes of the League. It's not too bad at all."

"Sorry. No can do. Big mouth," she explained, pointing at her lips. "I'd give away my thoughts in under two seconds. But I'll tell you what I'll do," she said, brightening up. "I'll take you away with me–far away from your nutty uncle and his crackbrained friends. We can forget all this–I promise not to mention it again–and we can get on with our plan."

"I can't do that to Uncle Henry. It would break his heart. You should see him fussing about me like a hen with her chick."

"Let me get this. You are giving up your chance of being liberated from your nightmare so that you can cross the meadow, because your uncle is behaving like some kind of bird? Is this what you're saying?"

"Well, not only that. We rather believe that crossing the meadow is not all that which we are given to understand. We fear that it might be a trap, and that by crossing it we may be giving up our right to resurrect."

"What happens," she said angrily, "is that 'we' are behaving like bloody idiots, believing all kind of fibs that wouldn't go down with a retarded child. I can't believe that I thought for a moment that you were made of the right stuff, and that we could be partners and get our mystery solved. If you want to get trapped in a make-believe world, suit yourself. I'll go on without you."

Clara stamped her foot, as if to seal her speech, turned away from him, and walked out quickly. George was left speechless, looking at her angry figure disappearing through the door.

The days passed, and George went on with his daily routine,

going to work in the morning and returning home in the early afternoon. He often took part in the tenant's meetings, where he enjoyed taking Mrs. Rothstein's side against the colonel. He and his uncle spent a lot of time together, and he tried to meet as many new people as possible. He also spent time with Agatha, who was always rushing to and fro, but who seemed to like George enough to stay put for the length of a friendly conversation with him, almost every day. The days passed quietly enough and, overall, George had no complaints. He had long since lost track of time, and this helped him to avoid any anxiety about the future. His only sorrow was that he missed Clara. She was often on his mind at the museum, in the long spells between visitors. He wished that she would find a way to come and live with his little community and be around. Almost every day he repressed the urge to go out and look for her, because he feared facing her anger again, and didn't know what else to say to her anyway.

Today he had left early. It was a national holiday and the museum was closed for the afternoon. George made it a point to leave always at the same time as Kim, and never earlier or later. The hours that were good enough for the living, he felt, should apply also to his visitors, if they wanted to keep the place running on reasonable rules. He walked briskly, eager to get home. The day before, Agatha and he had started planning the establishment of a new Entertainment Committee, which was shaping up quite well. He passed through the gates and was surprised to see Clara engaged in conversation with Uncle Henry near the entrance to the building.

"Hi, George," she said.

"Clara, what are you doing here?"

"I've come to take you with me. It's time to move on."

"We've been through this before," said George, eyeing Uncle Henry quickly, "and I told you that this is where I belong."

"Tell him, Henry," said Clara.

"They're pulling down the building," said Uncle Henry. "She heard them. They are coming tomorrow."

"Who are 'they'," asked George, confused.

"The City engineers," said Clara. "They are demolishing all the old buildings in this area. It's a part of the new plan for the city. They have already demolished one a couple of blocks from here, and tomorrow they are starting with this one. I overheard them talking about it, and I came to warn you. You've been playing this game long enough now, George. It's time to get back to reality and to keep going. And now that they will destroy this building it's the right time to go."

"But we'll find a new home. We'll move on to another one. There are enough buildings around." George felt lost at the thought of losing everything he had gotten accustomed to.

"Yeah? What will you do when they take that one down? Move to another one? And to another one? Wake up, George."

"Maggie won't move to another building," Uncle Henry said heavily. "She's staying here."

"What?" asked George. "But what about all that she's been preaching? The need to rationalize our lives, to be useful to society, to live in an organized manner?"

"Agatha's been talking to her for an hour now, but she won't budge. Let's go up and see what's happening."

They moved quickly up the stairs and into her bedroom. Maggie was lying on her bed and Agatha was sitting beside her, holding her hand.

"I'll tell you for the last time, Agatha. This is where I lived all my life, and this is where I'm staying. And I won't move simply because some clerk has decided to mess with our building. You can go, if you like."

"You know, Maggie, I always admired you for your strength. I knew that you were making up all those theories on continued life, but as long as you were there, preaching to us, it gave us a purpose, something to do and to look forward to. But if you fall apart, our community will not survive."

"I know, Agatha, but I no longer have the strength. They are going to destroy my last ties with this world, and I can't go on without them. Please forgive me. Now, if you don't mind," she said, her tone no longer apologetic, "I think that I will lie down here and wait for them."

She turned to one side and closed her eyes. The room suddenly felt empty, as Agatha got up and walked out. They followed her to the head of the stairs that led to the large room on the ground floor. The room was crowded with all the people that lived in the building. The colonel was there, side by side with Mrs. Rothstein and her two children. The young woman that reminded him of his dentist's secretary, and whose name he couldn't remember, was there, together with many others. They were looking up at Agatha, like lost children waiting for their school's headmaster to speak.

A man in the crowd gathered enough courage to ask her, "What's going on, Agatha? Is it true that they're going to demolish the building? And what is Maggie going to do about it?"

"It's true, my friend. The building will be destroyed

tomorrow morning. And Maggie, she's gone. She's no longer with us. We're on our own."

"Then I am taking charge now," said the colonel, "by virtue of rank and seniority. We need to organize and move to another building. A different building. Another one. I shall require order and obedience. This applies to everybody. To everybody it applies. Every one of you. Let's establish a new committee."

"Colonel," said Agatha, stopping him in mid-sentence. "The game is over. There is no 'we' anymore. No more committees, no more games. Finished. We've behaved like idiots for a long time now, playing around with our 'League' as if we could fool Death. Thank God it's over now, and we all understand that the prophecy was false. Please, let's keep whatever little dignity we have left."

A murmur of assent came from the crowd that was still keeping together, as if incapable of deciding what to do. The dentist's secretary stepped forward and climbed three stairs, turning to face the crowd.

"I don't know what you're going to do, folks, but I'm going to cross that meadow right now. So long. It has been nice meeting you all," she said, then stepped down, and walked out.

"George," Clara was now holding his hand and pulling him aside. "Will you come now? There is much to be done."

"Uncle," George looked inquiringly at Uncle Henry.

"What do you suggest, Agatha?" he asked.

"Well, Henry, I think that what that girl said was sensible enough. It's time for us to cross that meadow, and if it annihilates us, well, the world will be rid of two old nuisances."

"I'll come with you, Agatha," said Uncle Henry. "I, too, am tired of all this. Perhaps it's better this way. And you, my boy," he said, turning to George and hugging him briefly, "try not to get into any trouble and take good care of this girl. She deserves it. Let's go," he added to Agatha. "Maybe we can catch up with some of the boys."

Uncle Henry and Agatha were gone and the crowd had disappeared leaving only a few of the former League members moving in silence around the room, and the colonel who seemed rooted to his place.

"I'll miss the museum," said George.

"No, you won't. I've got a much better job for you. C'mon, let's get busy."

"You know, I'm glad that the City has decided to demolish this building. This was exactly what we needed to get back to reality and stop behaving like fools. A lot of people owe you for this. But how did you happen to hear about it?"

"I didn't," she said, laughing.

"Do you mean to say that you made that up? They're not going to demolish the building?"

"Well, they're probably going to do it soon, but not tomorrow. Innocent deception," she added apologetically. "Besides, this was the only way I could think of, to get you back. And it worked, didn't it?"

CHAPTER VIII
The Family

"Are you closing up, Berto?"

Alberto looked up at his boss Gerald, the hospital's acquisitions manager. He hadn't realized that it was so late. He had been working hard lately, knowing that Gerald was about to retire, and that he was in line for a promotion. He really needed the promotion to climb one difficult step up toward upper-middle-class status. "We may be able to get a new car soon," he had told his wife. A new car was not something to be taken for granted, with his salary as a government employee and his wife's modest income, which was all she could draw from the small family pharmacy in which she worked part-time together with her mother and brother.

"Yes. I'll be going soon too. But don't wait for me. I just want to balance these figures for the new beds we ordered, and I'll be gone."

He looked at the photographs on his desk. His wife, Maria, and his twin daughters, Silvia and Sandra–named after his wife's grandmothers–smiled back at him. He often looked at this photograph when he felt tired and discouraged. They were the reason why he worked so hard.

The girls were not identical twins. Silvia had black hair and green eyes, and moved with the self-confidence of a grown up. She often acted impulsively, but never stupidly. Sandra, in contrast to her sister, had brown hair and brown eyes, and a quiet, hesitant way of speaking and walking. Berto was always amazed to see how different they looked on occasions. He loved them both without limit, but for some reason felt the need to be more protective toward Sandra.

"You're overworking yourself, Berto," said Gerald. "There is a limit to the strain that you can take. I'm worried about you."

"Perhaps you're right, but I can't afford to miss getting my promotion when you retire."

"You know that I've recommended you for it. I'm sure that they will follow my recommendation."

"You know," said Berto, for a brief moment sounding unusually bitter, "sometimes I really despair at what my life has become. No matter how hard you work, you need luck and good connections to get somewhere. When I graduated *Summa cum Laude*, I thought that every big corporation would be more than lucky to have me, and I sat at home waiting for job offers to start pouring in. None came, of course, and after a while I understood that I had to start looking for a job. After five months of interviewing, I took this position. It was supposed to be a temporary job, and here I am, thirteen years later."

"It's not a bad place to work, here, after all," said Gerald.

"And you'll get the extra pay and benefits when you are promoted."

"I really need it, you know," said Berto, "if not for myself, at least for Maria."

"She's great, isn't she? I remember when you two met. I think you'd been working here for a few months."

"Yes, I met her at a friend's house. She had gone to school with his wife, and we happened to be invited for dinner together. And yes, she's really great. I'm certainly lucky. Maria is the best possible helpmate–loving and understanding. And she's given me two beautiful and adorable girls. I don't know what I would do without her."

"I'm glad that things are shaping up well for you, Berto. You deserve it. Don't you worry about that promotion. I'll talk to management again tomorrow, to make sure that they understand what an asset you are to the hospital. Now do yourself a favor, and go home."

"In a moment, thank you, Gerald. I really appreciate your help."

He forced himself to look at the figures that were dancing on the page in front of him. He would get home late tonight, as he had done almost every night in the last few months. Had it not been for Maria's encouragement, he could not have kept going. The thought of Maria brought a smile to his lips. "You stay on as much as you need, darling," she'd said. "You don't want anything to be in the way of your promotion."

Yes, he was definitely lucky to be married to such an understanding woman. Sometimes he felt as if he did not deserve her.

"I gotta go now. He could be back any moment."

Maria was lying on her side, naked, a cigarette between her lips. The man beside her made no attempt to stop her. He was rather happy to see her go. In fact, he wished she would be snappy about it. He didn't see the need to make such a production of getting out of bed and dressed.

"Well, if you must go, you must go," he said lightly.

He was satisfied now, and was looking forward to a quiet coffee and cigarette; and maybe later he would watch the sport news on TV. There was definitely no room for Maria in his plans for that evening.

His relationship with her had begun almost two years before. They had met during one of her interminable shopping days, at the department store where he worked as a floor manager. He had flirted with her, at first out of boredom, and then, when she had responded flirtatiously, with a real sense of adventure.

The first weeks of their affair had been breathtaking. Maria was demanding and childish, and requested his presence during shop hours. He had made excuses at work, in order to be able to meet her, and he lied at home to his wife, to answer Maria's calls. Life had become suddenly inebriating again for him, as in his puberty days, fueled by the fear of discovery and the fun of deceit.

Then his wife had been taken ill. Lung cancer, they had said, in an advanced stage. He had nursed her as best as he could, but he was a very poor helpmate for her. His wife had died slowly in her bed. It had taken her eight months, and many a time he had prayed for her quick death, sometimes because of self-pity, and more often in rage for her pain.

Maria did not seem to notice what was going on in his life. On the contrary, she had insisted in meeting him several times in his house–he no longer slept in the same room with his wife– tickled at the thought that she was in the room next to them. He had hated Maria for it, and had hated himself for being unable to resist her.

"I really don't feel like going home right now," said Maria. "It's the end of the month, and Berto always becomes a pest at this time. This is when he starts worrying about the future, the bank balance, and the cost of living. He irritates me with all his charts, expense analyses, and projections. You should see him when he tries to explain them to me," she said with scorn. "I don't understand them, and I don't care to try. But can you explain that to Berto? Not a chance. Back he comes every month with them, like a bad nickel, as if I had pleaded with him to show me."

"Well, tell him to piss off," said the man, with ill-concealed lack of interest.

"I wish I could," she said wistfully. "I've explained to him a million times that I don't want to hear about his charts, but does that get home to him, you think? Not at all."

At the time of his courtship, Berto had not seemed like a bad choice. He was nice and funny, and had potential. His friends thought the world of his intelligence, and she fully expected him to provide her with the happy and carefree kind of life that she deserved. Life was not an insurance policy, her mother used to tell her. Still, she considered that Berto had let her down real bad. None of his promises had materialized, and now it was too late to undo what had been done.

She was also entirely amoral, and had no remorse about cheating on her husband. For her this was a simple necessity, and her mother had taught her that you don't argue with necessities. You fulfill them. Moreover, keeping her affairs from him was for his own good. Actually, at times she thought that she was being commendably considerate in not letting him know. He suspected nothing and was happy. So, she asked herself, why not leave well enough alone?

And the girls? Well, she loved them, of course. In a way. Only she couldn't bring herself to worry too much about their future. What was there to worry about, anyway? Berto was doing enough worrying for all of them.

"Do you believe that pets go to heaven too, Sandra?"

"If they are good, I believe they do. Why?"

"I think I saw Browny today. He was walking along the corridor and I called to him, but he was gone. Do you think that it means that he's well?"

Browny was a small cat that Silvia had found in an alley near the house a few months earlier. It was only a kitten at the time, and she had brought it home. Her parents, at first, had refused to hear about keeping cats in the house. Tears and prolonged sobs had shaken their resolve, and she had been allowed to keep the kitten "for a few days," which had turned into weeks and then months. Then, one day, coming home from school they had found it dead in the backyard. It had fallen off the window ledge of the girls' room, and died instantly.

Silvia would not be consoled. All suggestions to replace Browny with a new kitten had been met by outraged refusals.

Browny was irreplaceable.

"I think you are being stupid!" Sandra had always been the more practical of the two. She had been just as sad as her sister at Browny's death. The first real encounter with death and its irreversibility had touched her no less than it had hit Silvia. But this had happened three weeks before, and life was going on. She saw no sense in keeping the mourning going on forever.

"I think you should forget about Browny and stop talking about him," she went on. "He's gone, and that's it!"

"How can you say such a thing? I will never forget Browny. Never! You go on and forget him, if you like!" Silvia got up and left the room, before her sister could see the tears coming back again.

Sandra was grateful that she had left. She would not have let Silvia see her own tears either. At any cost.

Berto walked home slowly, taking extra care not to bump into anything. It was late, but the fog was still there, engulfing the streets and hiding their contents. He wished it were summer again. He had always been nervous of the fog, and sometimes he was struck by an irrational, surging fear of it. He walked by the café where he used to have a quick morning coffee on his way to work. He had the strange feeling of being observed, although nobody was in sight. The lights were off and the doors were locked. Not many customers at this hour and in this weather, anyway. It was clever of them to close up and go home.

He quickened his pace, reaching for his key, readying himself to unlock the main door. The building used to have a night porter, many years ago, and a table still stood where he used to sit. But when the old porter had gone into retirement, the tenants had decided not to hire a new one. The janitor now doubled as a day porter, when he was around.

The key was old and bent and, as it sometimes happened, it would not turn. He had meant dozens of times to have a new key made, but had kept putting it off. In spite of the cold weather, sweat was now running on the back of his neck, while he fumbled with the key, trying to get in. At last, the key turned and he pushed the door, letting himself into the building. Berto was grateful for the comfortingly familiar and feeling of the badly lit hallway leading to the elevator. He was inside, and the world was outside, behind barred doors. He could breathe normally again.

"Turn off the lights, Berto," Maria said.

Berto never knew whether this was meant as an invitation to him or not. Their sex life during the last years had consisted of encounters that had become increasingly quick, dispassionate and far between; but this had been a blessing to him, since he was always so tired from work. Tonight, however, he was in the mood. He threw an arm around her, sliding closer to her body.

"I've got a headache, Berto. I have had a terrible day at the pharmacy, and I just need to get some sleep, okay?"

"Yeah," he said, trying to sound casual and not hurt. "I am tired too. Good night."

"Good night."

"Browny?"

Silvia woke up and sat on her bed. She was certain that she had heard something that sounded just like her kitten. He used to meow like that when he begged to come to bed with her. She looked around the room. Her sister was fast asleep in her bed, and she could hear the rhythmic sound of her breathing.

She listened attentively to the sounds of the house. None was coming from her parent's room. A very distant hum was coming from the roof, from the water system. She could always hear it when the air was still. Apart from that, the house was entirely silent. Still, she had heard a sound. She got out of bed and moved toward the window. A cat was standing on the windowsill, outside the closed window. He was walking back and forth, meowing at every other step, begging her to let him in.

"Browny, it's you!" she cried out loud.

She had no doubt that this was her kitten. His color was very distinctive, and she would recognize him anywhere—his voice, the way he wiggled his tail, they were unmistakable. The bond that had formed between them was so strong that she couldn't have been mistaken. He stopped when she came near and stood there, silent, with his head to one side, as if waiting for her to open the window and let him in. She debated for a moment whether to wake her sister up, and then decided against it. It would have been nice to be able to show her that she was right, that it was Browny coming to visit her, but the important thing now was to let Browny in. She knew that cats were not afraid of heights, but being out there was dangerous. She moved closer to him, raising her hand to unlock the window. Browny started fading away while she fought with the window locks, until he disappeared with a final, faint meow.

Sandra stirred and opened her eyes. Seeing her sister

standing by the window, she sat up and looked at her.

"What on earth are you doing out of bed at this hour?" she asked drowsily.

"Nothing. I thought I heard a noise in the street and got up to see what it was. But it was nothing. Go back to sleep."

Silvia climbed back into bed, and closed her eyes trying to remember what she just saw, unable to decide whether it had been real or a dream. Her sister was fast asleep again before Silvia even got under the sheets.

She decided eventually that she wouldn't tell anybody about Browny. They wouldn't believe her anyway, she concluded.

CHAPTER IX
The Park

Silvia and Sandra were playing in the park. They used to go there almost every day when it did not rain, to play and meet with friends. Often these would be new friends, children never seen before, passers-by, old people. Theirs was an age when making friends was easy.

The park was their playground, and they had grown to think of it as *their* park. Its eastern side led to the road, through an iron gate that was locked at night.

On the western side of the park, in shallow grounds, rested the ruins of a mediaeval tower that had once belonged to the inner walls of the city, now mostly crumbled away and only preserved at odd spots. Nothing much was left of what had once been an imposing building. A small gateway with a few iron bars protruding from its top led into a yard. Large stones that had tumbled from the top of the tower at some point of its life were scattered around.

At the other end of the yard a small opening made it possible to see a little pond outside, possibly the only remains of a once imposing lake. Many years ago a child had drowned in that pond. As a result, a fence had been erected, which would not be effective to keep anybody out, but was enough to enable the administrators of the park to disclaim responsibility for any new accident.

Silvia liked to come here and play in the yard. Sometimes she would convince Sandra to come and play with her, but most often she preferred to come alone, distancing herself from the shouts of the football game, or the duty of hide-and-seek routines that bored her quickly. Then she would dream of herself as a princess, and tell herself a story that never repeated itself. At one time she would be imprisoned in the tower by an enemy of her father, the King, and a prince would come and rescue her, fighting bravely against the Black Soldiers. On other occasions she would be a warrior princess, coming to the rescue of people in peril. Her sister, Sandra, was sometimes allowed to join in her daydreaming, usually in the role of the victim to be rescued, and sometimes as a member of her army, but she was never allowed a principal role in her fables.

Silvia liked to daydream. She was good at it, and the worlds she created were as vivid to her as the real world, as long as the dream went on. But her worlds were also much better than reality. The people in it were better, stronger, and nicer or, if they were bad, they always found their match in her. But the daydreaming was particularly good to her, because she was in command. She decided what would happen; she would make it rain or shine, and she prevailed over the forces of evil. She was doing a much better job in her worlds than grown-ups were doing in real life, she thought. So why not spend as much time as possible in a better place?

Today she had left Sandra with some new friends, playing volleyball on the grass.

"Are you coming to play with us?" Sandra had asked her.

"Maybe later," answered Silvia, for the benefit of the others. She knew that Sandra was not really expecting her to come.

"Okay," said Sandra with a shrug, and walked away.

Silvia didn't feel like playing, but rather was eager to continue her last daydream. On her last visit to the tower she had been in the middle of an expedition launched to save a particularly handsome prince from the hands of a witch who had taken him to be her servant. Her sister, calling to her to come home, had abruptly interrupted her fantasy. It was strange, but she was never able to continue a dream started in the yard, at home or elsewhere. This was the place for dreaming, and she had to come back here, if she wished to complete her fantasy. And she had to, because an unfinished one would irk her every day, and make her restless.

A low, thick mist covered the yard. It was of the type that clings to your ankles but seems incapable of rising to higher levels. The mist rose from the small pond and reached the open space within the yard, hiding small obstacles on the ground. Silvia stumbled on a piece of wood and almost fell. A sharp pain ran through her leg, and she stood for a while, fighting back tears unfit for a warrior princess. This was the witch's doing, she decided, and motioned to her warriors to come and protect her while she dealt with her deep, but not mortal wound.

At first she did not notice the woman sitting on the stone at the edge of the yard, watching her play. Silvia started her daydream by imagining her soldiers moving around in the yard. She had to replay some of the final scenes of her last dream, because during the week, while the rain had kept her inside, she had thought of many ways in which they could be improved upon. Here was someone looking after a wounded comrade, and there was someone else fetching water. Movement was also coming from above her head–she imagined–from the railed stone steps that ran up to the head of the tower. The yard was now bustling with activity, with warriors coming and going, and fair lady warriors helping the wounded. One of the women was not acting her part, though. Instead of rushing to and fro like the others, she only sat there, motionless.

She stared at the woman. She could not remember having created her. She was wearing a long dress, almost a nightgown, and had a small, pale face framed by long black hair. She was smiling a narrow smile, but was not taking any part in the events of the battle. She seemed to be out of place there. Suddenly she realized that the woman sitting in front of her was not at all her creation, nor a part of her dream.

"Wow!" Silvia said. "You scared me."

"Don't be scared. I was just watching you." She had a deep, throaty voice.

"I must have looked pretty silly to you, didn't I?"

"Not at all. I guess you were playing, weren't you?"

"Yes, I was being princess Ethelberta, and I was saving young prince Yuli from a bad witch. I read a story about them, and I thought they were cute."

"Do you come here often?"

"Yes. I like to come here to play."

"So did I. I liked to come to this part of the park and sit here, with the sun in my face. This is a very quiet place. But now I don't come here too often."

"Why?"

"There is no point."

Silvia was taken aback by her answer, and by the sadness that she sensed in this woman.

Silvia's need for knowledge was insatiable and she dealt with it simply by asking whatever question she had in mind. As her father used to say, she asked people questions "regardless of sex and age." Many a time her parents had had to apologize to strangers who were asked about their physical peculiarities, or the poor state of their shoes, or any other awkward question that Silvia could come up with. "But, Daddy," she used to argue, "how am I to know the answer if I don't ask the question?" She had never accepted the simple explanation that there are certain questions that you just don't ask. "If they don't like the question," she would maintain obstinately, "they can simply refuse to answer."

This lady looked unhappy to her; her eyes were sad, and Silvia had to know why.

"Why are you sad?" she asked with childish candor.

"It's a long story. I will tell you, but first tell me about yourself. Tell me about your mother."

"My mother?" Silvia repeated in surprise. "There is nothing special about my mother. She just–she's my mother."

"What does she do now?"

"She works in a pharmacy, helping Granny, same as she has always done." Silvia had the uncomfortable feeling that she should not be answering these questions. But then, this collided with her own approach to life. If *she* were allowed to ask any question, why wouldn't this lady also be permitted to ask *her*? She decided that she would simply not answer any question that sounded too personal to her.

"I know your mother, you know? I think that she would like to hear that the two of us had met. Will you tell her?"

This looked like a very odd lady to Silvia, and one that must be a little funny in the head, because although she said that she knew her mother, Silvia had never seen her before. Nevertheless, she knew by experience that grown-ups who act strangely should be humored. It was like her uncle who came often to visit them from the country; she could never understand what he was talking about, but he seemed very happy to have her answer "Yes," and "Of course," every now and then, to punctuate his long and meaningless speeches. She decided that this strange lady should also be humored, as long as it didn't cost her anything.

"Of course I'll tell her, if you like. What's your name?"

"My name is not important. Tell your mother that you have met the other woman. You tell her that I heard everything from the other room. Tell her that I am not quite gone yet, and that I am watching my husband, all the time. Will you tell her this?"

Silvia had been taught not to talk to strangers; she had been told that strangers might be dangerous. They might be crazy people, maniacs, killers. This strange lady could be one of them. She started thinking that perhaps she should simply turn around and run away. She also remembered her father's instructions never to take messages from people who telephoned and refused to identify themselves. And she was not liking this lady much, funny or not funny in the head.

"If you don't tell me your name, I won't tell my mother anything at all," Silvia said defiantly.

"Oh yes, you will," the woman said, menacingly.

"No. I won't. And I don't believe that you know my mother either," she added.

"I know your mother very well, Silvia."

"How do you know my name? I never told you!"

"I know a lot about you; and about your sister, Sandra. I know you much better than you imagine," said the woman. "I know your kitten, Browny, and I know how he died because you didn't take good care of him. You know, he suffered a lot before he died. And it was your fault, all your fault!"

Her face was now contorted in an expression of hatred such as Silvia had never seen before. She got up and took a step toward Silvia, menacingly. Silvia was suddenly scared of this weird woman who knew her name and said strange things. She didn't know what to do. To turn and run? To call for help?

She started walking backwards, afraid of turning, afraid the woman might leap and grab her.

"Yes, walk away, Silvia," said the woman with a smirk pasted all over her face. "Go tell your mother that the woman in the other room has not forgotten. Tell her that I do not forgive her. Tell her!"

Silvia quickened her backward walk, a fear never experienced before gripping at her throat. The woman did not seem to be attempting to follow her, and she was now already outside the gate of the tower, in the comfort of the open space. Suddenly a hand fell on her shoulder, causing her heart to leap to her throat, and her to spin around, to face Sandra.

"Silvia! Are you dreaming? I've been calling you for hours!"

Silvia was relieved to see her. She often felt that, in time of distress, the two of them were one, and the presence of her sister was a real source of strength to her. She turned around to face the woman, feeling now safe again.

She was not there.

"Where has she gone?" she asked.

"Where has who gone?"

"The woman I was talking to. The woman that was sitting on that stone," Silvia said, pointing at the stone in the yard.

"There was nobody here. I saw nobody. You must've been dreaming."

"No. She was here, I talked to her."

Sandra shook her head slowly, weary of the argument, and pulled her sister by the sleeve.

"Come on, we must go back. We are late already."

They walked slowly toward the gates. Silvia stopped a few times to look back, but nobody was in the yard.

"Sandra–" she started.

"Yes? What is it?"

"Didn't you see me talking with that lady? Didn't you hear me?"

"Of course I heard you. I heard you saying, 'How do you know my name? I never told you!' but, of course, it was all in your daydream, 'cause there was nobody there. I saw you move your hands as if in conversation and I saw you walking backwards, and I wondered what kind of story you were cooking up. What was it?"

"Never mind," Silvia said weakly.

She resolved not to tell her mommy anything, knowing she wouldn't be believed, anyway.

Actually, Silvia herself did not know what to believe.

That night she lay in her bed, crying silently for Browny. She didn't believe that horrible woman; still, it could have been her fault. It surely was her fault. She had not watched out for her little kitten. She tried to remember it moving around the house, sleeping on her pillow and playing with her shoelaces.

I can't remember him clearly, she wept silently. I am forgetting him, and if I forget, I can't keep him alive.

That night she cried herself to sleep, the woman from the park completely forgotten in her struggle to remember.

CHAPTER X
The Apartment

The apartment was dark, and everybody was asleep. The time was close to midnight when Clara and George stood in the small hallway and looked around. His father had kept in the hall a large painting of a medieval battle scene, with lots of blood and severed heads. It was a very valuable work of art, he remembered, and he was told off every time he went near it. He had hated that painting, because it was so good that the people in it looked real to him. He used to fear that they would jump off the canvas and come after him, and used to spend a lot of time looking at them, to make sure that they weren't moving. Once, he watched the picture for too long and fancied that the cavalier in the black armor had moved. From that moment on, going to sleep had never been the same. The painting had to be checked and a head count taken, and the bed had to be inspected, above and below, to ensure that no black knight was hiding anywhere. It was on one such evening, he now remembered, that Clara had come and sat with him until he had fallen asleep, holding her hand as his shield against black cavaliers. He looked at her now, feeling a real wave of affection toward this poor, tormented girl.

George now looked at the wall, half expecting to see the painting there. Instead, the ugliest framed tapestry ever had taken its place. It was of a particularly repulsive design, showing a hunting scene the type that you can buy at a charity sale.

"Give me a minute, will you?" he said. Their apartment had a separate dining room that was connected with the kitchen via a small service window. He stepped into the room and, for a second, felt as if he had gone back in time. His father had sold most of the furniture together with the apartment, and the dinner table had been left behind, together with the set of chairs that went with it. The table and the chairs stood there, in the middle of the room, just as he had left them on the day of their departure. The room was small, and there was no space for anything else in it. The pictures on the walls had been replaced, but the ones put in their place by the new owners were not dissimilar from the ones that had once hung there. The illusion of having gone back in time was almost perfect.

He sat on the chair that had been his for so long, on the left-hand side of his father who always sat at the head of the table. His mother had sat at his father's right. He let his mind wander, back to those happier days and the quiet meals they used to enjoy here. But had those indeed been happier days, he wondered? He was not so sure any more. He remembered the tension in the room, created by his father's presence. His father had had this effect on most people, but particularly on him, and especially during meals. He was not a clumsy child, but he remembered the embarrassment of spilling a drink, or the salt, as could happen to anybody, and the cold stare from his father that would follow any transgression of what he categorized as "good behavior". No, he was not at all sure that those were happy days. But then how come he had missed them, and had told himself for years how good they had been? Denial, he decided. That is what you do when you don't want to remember how unhappy you had been. This is why nations re-write history, to cancel the shame of a lost war or of the disgraceful behavior of their sons.

"You coming?" He raised his head at the sound of Clara's voice. She was standing in the doorway, looking at him pensively.

"Did you use to have meals here, when you lived with us?" he asked.

"Yes, sometimes. At least, at the beginning."

"And where would you sit then?"

"At the other end of the table, in the chair beside you."

Thank God, he thought somewhat irrationally, that at least he did not seat her in Mother's chair.

"And how was I during the meals?"

"Quiet—very quiet—and polite. I remember thinking that you were the politest kid I had ever met. You never spoke unless one of us addressed you first. You always said 'please' and thanked us for everything. But you were old enough to remember those meals. Don't you?"

"Not much. Barely. Perhaps they were too boring for me." George sat musing for a while, trying to remember, but he could only evoke sporadic pictures of himself sitting at the table. He couldn't remember Clara eating with them. Not at all.

"Shall we get going now?" she asked again.

"Yes. Let's." He got up, feeling lighter.

They started moving along the corridor.

"This way to the bathroom," he said.

"I know," she answered, "but let's take a look at the family and see whether they are awake."

They turned left, and stood at the door of the twins' bedroom.

"Shh," she said. "We must be careful not to scare them. Children sometimes can feel us, and maybe see us. I don't know. They are much more perceptive than grown-ups."

It indeed appeared that Silvia had felt something.

"Browny! Is it you?" she cried. "Where are you? Come here."

They receded back into the darkness, afraid that she might see them.

"You see?" she whispered. "She has felt our presence."

"It may be a coincidence."

"Keep your voice down," Clara whispered the order. "She might hear you."

"Sandra, Sandra. Get up!" Silvia called. Her sister stirred, opened an eye, and looked at her.

"What's the matter? Why are you up again?"

"I've heard something," Silvia said, deciding not to tell her sister that she believed it could be Browny again, "and I don't want to go alone and see. Come with me."

"Where?"

"In the hallway. There was a sound and I think I saw a shadow, as if someone was walking there."

"Stop it! You are giving me the creeps. I'm going to wake Daddy."

"No you aren't!" Silvia said, decisively.

"But it could be burglars, or something." Sandra was fully awake now, and started to grow agitated.

"Well, if it is a burglar, we will yell for Daddy. Now let's go and take a look."

They walked into the corridor and stood near the door to their room, from which they could see all of it. They could not see the two shadows hiding in the darkness of the dining room into which they had retreated.

"You see? There's nobody here," Silvia said. "I'm glad that we didn't wake Daddy up for nothing. Let's go back to bed."

The girls climbed back into bed, yawned, and curled up under the sheets. Silence fell onto the room, from which only the regular breathing of the girls came.

"I think that the girls have gone back to sleep," Clara said. "Let's go on."

They went farther down the corridor, passing again before the door leading into the girls' bedroom. Silvia opened her eyes cautiously. She had not been able to go back to sleep, and had the feeling that something was going on now. Perhaps Browny was back again. She saw what she had thought she had seen before, two shadows moving quickly along the corridor, cast for a brief instant on the wall by the small light that burned between their beds, near the door. She caught a glimpse of them, and they were gone.

She decided she was imagining things. Nobody was there and she'd better go back to sleep. She closed her eyes again, and soon the regular sound of her breathing was matching that of her sister's.

George turned into the master bedroom, followed by Clara.

This was the where his parents had slept and was the largest room in the house. The room in front had been used by his father as a study, and was now a playroom for the twins. Maria and Berto were in bed, fast asleep. They were facing away from each other, not touching. George felt a pang of pain at the waste of people sleeping apart, and spending their best years being distant.

Maria was turning now, and reached out for Berto, throwing her hands around him. Berto woke up, looking surprised but not complaining, and reached out to hug her tightly.

"You did it!" George stated as a fact. "You are messing around with other people's intimate moments. This is much worse than my little prank on the tram."

"I did it to wake them up a bit," Clara said. "What's the point of our being here to make noises if there's nobody awake enough to hear? And besides, they look much nicer now, don't you think?"

"All right. You want to make noises, so let's go make noises. You first."

"Don't you want to stay here for a moment and see what happens?"

"I am surprised at you, young lady," he said. "I am not a voyeur, and I am not interested in other peoples' sexual activities. Please remain and watch, if you find it entertaining, but I still retain some decency, and I will wait outside."

"Come on, George, don't be a stuffed shirt. I just thought that I might be able to help them along, if needed, but they seem to be doing fine without my help," she added when the sheets went flying off the bed. "No need to stay now. Let's get down to work."

They left the room, went into the bathroom, and looked around. Nothing had changed since he had last used it. The same tub, the same faucets, and the same tiles. It looked like yesterday.

"You said that you wanted to create noises, but what the point is now, I don't know. They are so busy, thanks to you I may add, that they wouldn't hear a band if it played here in the bathroom." George was irritated. His irritation had started on their way to the apartment, and had grown ever since. He felt utterly impotent to influence the course of events, and he needed someone to blame. He knew it was not fair to blame her for all of it, but she was the only one around. And he was also mad at Clara. He did not think that her plan had a chance of success, and whatever slim chances they had were jeopardized, so he felt, by her frivolous approach to their expedition. Here they were, working against all odds, and she taking time to foster these peoples' sex life, and what's more, she was enjoying it. He was not at all a puritan, but she was blemishing the image of her that he had built in his mind, and he was angry with her for it.

"Noises won't help if they don't see some actual evidence that something is wrong with the water system. This calls for a greater effort than just noises." She sounded unconvincingly matter-of-fact. This was not the right time to pick a fight, they both knew that.

"I'll start by making a little water drip from the faucet." She concentrated, and soon a little drop of water appeared in the tub. The result was unimpressive.

"I don't think that I can do much better than that. This is difficult enough, but perhaps I can get some water to wet the floor."

Clara concentrated again, and a little pool of water appeared on the floor, at the edge of the tub. The drops in the tub were now making a low but annoying "drip, drip" noise.

She looked at George, and studied his face. "Don't be mad at me. Please. I know that I'm being a little silly every now and then, but the truth is that this is the first time in years that I am actually having fun. You know, I could've gone into any house every day, but I never did. I never felt like it, until you came along. Therefore, in a sense, it's all your fault that I'm feeling good enough to be able to enjoy myself. I mean no harm to anybody. Please, don't spoil the fun. This may be the last time I can have any."

George felt disarmed. She was right; she was entitled to feel happy for a while and he had no right to take this away from her.

"I'm sorry. I am not really mad at you. It's just—maybe I need some more time to get adjusted. I'll do my best not to interfere. I'll even try to help. I'll turn on the lights," he said, "otherwise he'll miss the pool."

"Do you think that you can do it?"

"I think so. I don't know why—but then I know nothing at all, anyway."

He was startled to realize that he also was beginning to enjoy their expedition. Here he was, an untouchable voyeur, touring somebody else's house and playing tricks on him. He had not always been the respectable bore he was now. He, too, had once been a child, and had been responsible for his share of pranks. He was feeling fifteen again, experiencing the same elation that comes from doing forbidden acts, but without the fear of discovery and retribution. He could do this simply for the fun of it.

He concentrated on the lights. He had not tried this before, but had a feeling that it could be done. He pictured to himself his hand touching the switch and turning it up. And the lights came on.

"Great!" Clara said. "Now let's go and fetch them."

They went back to the bedroom and stopped at the door. Unmistakable sounds were coming from within.

"What are they doing?" Clara asked petulantly.

"What do you think they are doing? You started it."

"Well, I'm going in."

She took him by the hand, and in a moment they were in the bedroom. Maria and Berto were now lying in a satiated embrace, talking in whispers.

"That was good," Maria was saying. "We should be doing this more often."

"I love you, Maria," said Berto.

"Mmm," mumbled Maria, noncommittally.

"I said I love you," Berto repeated, a little louder.

"Yeah," said Maria.

"We shouldn't be here," George said. "It doesn't feel right to intrude on them like this."

"We are dead, remember? Sex doesn't mean a thing to us."

"Well, you certainly don't act like it. Making her start the whole thing, and now peeping like this."

Clara was about to reply, when Berto got up and said, "I'm going to the bathroom. I'll be right back."

He walked quickly toward the bathroom, and stopped at the door.

"Maria," he called. "Have you left the lights on?" Leaving lights on was something he particularly abhorred. A pure waste of money, it was.

"And what's this?" he asked Maria, who had joined him in the bathroom.

"There is water on the floor, and the tap is dripping. One could slip here and break a leg."

He dried the floor with a towel and turned the tap tightly. He then switched off the lights, and they both went back to bed.

George and Clara stood in the bathroom in silence, not looking at each other.

"Great results we've got here," he finally said. "We have really managed to scare them into having sex. Perhaps if we do this every night, they'll take more showers and in fifty years they will *have* to change the tub. Is that the plan?"

"All right. That wasn't too impressive, I admit," she said. "But, perhaps, if we do this every night they'll have to take notice and do something about it."

"Give me a break! Even if we manage to wet their floor with two drops of water every night–which seems to be the best we can accomplish–they'll never take the hint and replace the bathtub. Why should they? Do you really think that you can make them take trips to the bathroom every night? No, this isn't the way to go. If you want to go on making a nuisance of yourself, please be my guest, but count me out."

She didn't argue. She no longer looked as if she minded his sarcasm. It was clear now that this wasn't going to work if George had decided not to help her.

"We will have to think of something else," she said with downcast eyes.

Irritation was mounting in him again. He couldn't understand why he had let her convince him to undertake a useless enterprise based on such a far-fetched assumption. It was clear to him that all their so-called powers had no real effect on living people. They were kidding themselves if they thought that something could be accomplished in that way. It had been only a waste of time, he thought, and the only result had been to make him feel silly.

"Well, when you do, let me know. Meanwhile, I'll see you around," he said, and left through the hall, leaving Clara alone to contemplate the ruins of her plan.

CHAPTER XI
Friends

"Pardon me, sir," said the old woman. "I am looking for my husband. I have lost him somewhere in this garden, and I can't find him. He must be worrying himself sick about me. He knows I can't manage without him."

George looked at her. She was staring straight at him, in expectation of an answer.

He wondered if she were alive or dead but as she was talking to him, he concluded that she must be dead. Living people could not see him. He knew this for a fact, after having walked the streets of the city for a long time. The old woman did not seem to be aware of her condition, though, and he stood there, undecided on how to answer her. He did not like the idea of being the one to tell her what had happened to her.

"Can you show me where the water fountain is, sir?" she continued. "I have been walking around the garden for a long time now, and I'm very thirsty. I think I can hear the water running."

George was standing beside a fountain that gave a little water. And she was looking directly at it.

He realized, with a shock, that she was blind, and that she could sense his presence. But she was alive. Not for the first time he resented the unfairness of his situation—he was excluded from this world, but got to touch it at unexpected times.

"The fountain is straight ahead of you, ma'am," he said quietly, as if afraid to scare her, "just a few paces straight ahead."

"Thank you, young man, God bless you," said the woman, moving toward the fountain. She reached it and drank avidly. She wetted her face that was red and congested by the heat, and then took a handkerchief from her purse and wiped it.

He watched her and waited, unwilling to be rude and go away, although he knew that this would have been the sensible thing to do.

"How did you know that I am young?" he asked.

"When you are my age, anyone who can walk around unaided is young," she said simply.

George took immediately to this old woman, who spoke simply and plainly. He wished he could do something for her.

"When did you part from your husband, ma'am?" he asked.

"Oh, it must have been at least two hours ago. He was going to read poetry to me, you know. We have been doing this, here in the garden, for over sixty years now," she added, almost apologetically. "We come here and sit in the sun, and he reads out loud to me. Neither weather nor war have been able to keep us away from this garden."

She was smiling now, taking pleasure at the thought, and

perhaps looking forward to the coming treat. Then she continued, in a somber tone.

"He told me, 'Just a second, honey. I'll be right back. Don't go away', and left. And he hasn't come back.

"I am not worried, of course," she continued hastily, as if to chase away a bad thought. "He would never leave me. Even when our neighbor, who was ten years younger than me, started to flirt with him, I wasn't worried–she is dead now, you know, and I don't want to speak ill of the dead, but she has tried for years to steal him away from me. When I spoke to him about it, he just laughed and said, 'She is younger, but you are much more beautiful, and I'm no fool'.

"I know my husband, that's why I'm not worried. But I don't understand what's keeping him so long. Do you think he may have forgotten to come back? He is not young, you know. He is almost ninety. Sometimes he forgets things."

"Maybe he has gone to fetch something, perhaps the book he was going to read from," George said, trying to sound convinced.

"Oh, I don't know. He didn't say anything. I tried to while away the time with poetry, but all I could remember is something I learnt in school many years ago. Perhaps you know it? It goes,

Seven pairs of shoes I have worn out
All made of iron,
While looking for you;

Seven sticks of iron I have consumed
To support me,

Along my fateful way;

Seven flasks of tears I have filled,
Seven long years
Of bitter tears;

You sleep at my desperate cries,
And the rooster crows,
But you would not wake up.

There was sadness in her recitation. George understood why. He, too, had learnt this fable in school, and he knew it had no happy ending. She knew that her husband was not going to read poetry to her again, and she was sharing her sadness with him—the sadness of a proud woman who cannot admit that her life, as she knew it, has come to an end.

She stood there silent, as if savoring the intimate moment that had passed between them. Then she spoke again.

"Can you now please tell me if you have seen my husband?"

"I fear I have seen nobody around here. It would be better for you to sit down and wait. He is bound to come back. Or someone is sure to come along."

She sat on a stone ledge beside the fountain. It was amazing, he thought, to see how naturally she moved around without the help of eyesight.

"Can't you go and look for him?" she asked, sounding pleading for the first time.

"I am afraid that I can't, much as I would like to. I have to go now. But please, do as I suggest. Sit here, and someone will come along soon."

She lifted her chin defiantly, and waved her hand, as if to signify that she did not care one way or the other.

"You are all the same," she said acidly. "Nobody can spare a minute to help an old woman who is lost. Everybody is in a hurry to go and make more money, as if that mattered in the end. You should be ashamed of yourself," she said, slowly. "Now go away, please. I have no use for the likes of you."

She turned her back to him, and sat there, in silence. There was nothing George could do or say. He walked quickly away, feeling ashamed. He almost stopped and turned back to explain, to excuse himself to her. But there was no simple explanation. At least, not one that he cared to offer.

He walked down a gravel path leading deeper into the garden, hurriedly, to get away from her as quickly as possible. At the bottom of the path he turned around to look at the old woman. She was still sitting there, tight-lipped as he had left her, her back straight, and waiting for help to come along.

George had been looking for Clara everywhere. Then he had waited for her at the café, and when she hadn't come, he had gone out, looking for her again. And here she was, sitting on a stone bench behind an ancient palace. Two large bushes of mixed greenery almost completely hid her from the view of passers-by. The wind moved the bushes a little, quietly, almost hesitantly.

George wondered if she were hiding from him. She was certainly not hiding from living persons who could not see her, and the place was deserted anyway. So she must be hiding from him, he concluded.

She was wearing a T-shirt and jeans; an outfit that made her look even younger than the dress she had worn when they first met. He had been wondering about the change of clothing lately, noting that his own shirt and pants never remained the same for long. He had harbored the notion for a while, that this might be a dream. The only reasonable explanation of his sorry state was that he had been dreaming throughout, and would soon wake up, get dressed and go to work. But he had given up pretending after a while.

Maybe we are not real, and what we wear is not real, and it changes when our mood changes, he thought, and maybe nothing of this is real—the palace, the bench, her hair—

But Clara looked real enough to him. In fact, she had never looked so real. She was hiding her face in her hands, and either was unaware of his presence, or was ignoring him.

"May I sit down?" he asked.

Clara lifted her head and looked at him. Her eyes were wet with tears, as if she had been crying for a long time. She opened her mouth, as if to speak, and then merely nodded and lowered her head again.

George had never seen her in such a state. "What happened? What's the matter?" he asked with concern. She didn't answer, and he sat by her and took her hands in his. "Tell me," he half-ordered and half-begged.

"I'm scared," she said. "I've never been so scared since—since then."

"What are you afraid of?" he asked, adding with a feeble attempt at a joke, "We are dead, remember? We are the ones who are supposed to scare the others. You got your wires crossed."

She showed no sign of being comforted by his joke, but

shrugged and went on.

"I thought–I thought that once you are dead, no more harm can come to you. 'What's worse than death?' I asked myself. Now I know that there are worse things than death."

"Like what?"

"Like being stuck over here, uncertain of tomorrow. Not knowing how long this will go on. Not knowing if it will ever end. And like..." she hesitated, then stopped.

"What else?" George asked.

"Hold my hand now, and press a little. Yes, like this. Can you feel me?"

"Yes I can. And a good feeling it is!"

"Don't joke! I 'm serious."

"Okay, I promise. I'll be serious."

"Just before you came now, I lost the sense of touch for a while. It has come back to me now, but for a short while I thought I'd lost it forever. I touched my hand, and could feel nothing. I touched my hair, and it was as if I wasn't there. I felt that I was–how to explain–vanishing."

"This is silly, you know," George said softly. "I don't even know that we are supposed to have a sense of touch. Do you know that I have the sense of smell? I can smell things, but it seems different than it used to be. And I ask myself, 'Am I entitled to a sense of smell?' It may well be an oversight of someone up there, and I go about in fear that He may find out and take the smells away from me. What will I do next? Perhaps we are supposed to learn to live–I use the term in a loose sense– without smelling anything."

"I'm scared," Clara said, and she definitely looked it, "because I don't understand what's happening to me. Perhaps the ones who can't cross the meadow are damned to vanish after some time, and never make it to the other side? Perhaps this–being here–is our punishment, and not only a transient state? I don't know.

"I have tried to understand more. I tried to talk to a keeper at the meadow, once, when I felt undecided and I thought that, maybe, I should cross. But you have heard how little use it is talking to them. She could have been the same one you met."

"Didn't she answer your questions?"

"Oh yes, she did, and she explained at length–and much of what I know, I owe to her. However, most of her explanations were unclear to me. Some had no meaning at all, and others were ambiguous."

"We have no control over any of this, I am afraid. It only looks as if we can decide when to cross the meadow, but in fact we can't go before we're ready for it," said George, and then continued, changing the subject. "I've been looking for you for quite some time now. To apologize for having been rude, up there in the apartment, and to tell you that we must renew our efforts and find a way to solve our common mystery. Maybe if we do, we can really get out of here."

"You know, when I was a lot younger–"

"You are young; you still are a young girl. And you're beautiful." He was trying to comfort her, but he was also saying things he had been trying to say for a long time.

"I must say that I am a little jealous of my father. I know I shouldn't be, and that's kind of weird and creepy, but I envy him for having had your company and your affection."

"You are much better than him," Clara said in a low, quiet voice. "You are kinder, and gentler. I could have fallen in love with you back then." She was clearly trying to comfort him back.

"Yeah, you could have, I guess," George said, pensively.

They sat without speaking for a while. Then she sat up and looked at him.

"Do you know what I would like to do now?"

"No. Tell me."

"I would like to drink a soda."

"That sounds exciting enough."

"No, I'm serious. I would like to hold a cold soda in my hand, and drink it slowly. The problem is that, even if I could hold a soda in my hand, I'm not thirsty any more. I haven't been thirsty for years. And I think that thirst could make me feel alive again. Even pain could. Anything."

"I try not to give too much thought to old bad habits like drinking, you know. You shouldn't harp on it. It's morbid. Better try to distance yourself."

She eyed him with a pensive glance and her shoulders sagged a little bit more. George sensed that she was cracking and wouldn't be able to endure this for much longer.

He sat there, quiet, not knowing what to say next.

"Do you think I am attractive?" Clara asked after a while.

"Attractive? You must be kidding. You are gorgeous."

"Do you really think so?"

"Look. I never thought that I could get near a girl as beautiful as you. In real life I would have probably chickened out at the mere idea of talking to you. Do I think you are attractive, you ask me? I call that fishing for compliments."

She became pensive again. The day was wearing on, and the palace was now casting long shadows in front of them. The wind drew low hums from between the marble columns that framed the palace.

A dog appeared from behind the palace. It was sniffing the ground, obviously looking for mesmerizing scents left by other dogs. At about twenty paces from them it stopped, looked in their direction, and started to howl. It pressed its belly to the ground and turned around, disappearing around the corner, its cry turning into a high-pitched whimpering.

We are unwelcome in this world, George thought. I must say that I have started to dislike it myself.

Clara shivered, as if feeling cold, although the cold could no longer affect her.

"George," she said, looking straight at him. "Will you hold me for a while? Please?" she added quickly, as if sensing his embarrassment.

"Come here," he said, throwing his arms around her. She was surprisingly small, and her body felt light, almost as if she were not there. They remained in a close embrace for a while, her head resting on his shoulder with her face buried into his neck. He could not say whether she was crying or only resting there. Her hand moved along his back, massaging his neck and pulling him closer and closer. His hand now also started to move, as if by a reflex of her movement. Her blouse was short and his hand encountered the flesh of her back. It felt soft, but different from the feeling of skin that he remembered. It felt more like a sponge; far less consistent than flesh. He moved his hand slowly along her back, then stopped and moved gently away from her, still holding her in his arms.

"I'm sorry," he said, lowering his eyes. "I really am; but I don't feel anything. It doesn't make anything stir in me. I guess my body–whatever it is–just doesn't function. It's not your fault. It's me."

"Don't worry. I feel the same. I guess that's who we are now." She sighed and let her arms fall.

"This doesn't mean that I don't care about you, you know? I do. Very much."

"I know. I can feel that much. I'm sorry that I was so stupid. I thought that, if I were still able to make a man take an interest, it would make me feel more alive. And I do care about you too, so that it was not difficult to try. Only it doesn't work, right? Please forget it."

Clara was blushing now, like an adolescent on a first date, and she looked younger and even more beautiful than before.

"You know, holding you in my arms is no great hardship either," George said. "I rather think that I would like to keep this up for a while. Maybe my hormones are dead, but it still feels good."

"Do you mind if I lay my head on your knees, then?"

"Not at all. By all means do."

"Thanks," she said, putting her feet on the bench and looking up at him. "This is really comfy, you know?"

"It is just my luck, you see? The one time that I have a beautiful young girl all to myself in a romantic garden, all I can do is talk."

"You know, when I was young–"

"And it's not as if I weren't interested, I mean. You are not ugly, pimpled, or hunchbacked. Quite the contrary–"

"As I was trying to say when you stopped me with your frivolous comments," she continued with a smile, but one that seemed forced, "when I was much younger, a teenager, I always dreamt of a male friend, a good friend with whom I could talk, and hold hands, and feel warm and secure and comfortable. But all my friends wanted only one thing, Sex. And that always spoiled our friendship. No friendship ever survived the sex. Now I may have found what I have always looked for. And you know what? I feel like a teenager again."

"You certainly have made *me* feel like a teenager. But you are damn right, I am your friend, and I hope you feel secure and comfortable with me."

"Yes, I do. Do you?"

"The truth?"

"Only the truth."

"I am glad that sex is out of the question. I don't know that I could have resisted the temptation, and that would have ruined everything. And it feels good being with you now." A reassuring thought occurred to him, "You know, this can't be such a bad world, after all, if whoever is running it is letting us get together and support one another."

"Don't go philosophic on me now, please, George. The two things that I need most right now are your sense of humor, and my sense of touch."

They sat in silence, watching the shadows getting longer and longer, as the evening crept in. They held hands, and they touched each other, and felt almost alive. Each fell into private thoughts that they did not feel like sharing.

But they did feel comforted.

CHAPTER XII
The Teacher

George was sitting on a wooden bench in the garden near the café. He had been sitting there, he could not figure out for how long, but he knew it had to be a long time, because he had seen at least two sunrises since getting there.

In his mind, he was going through his last conversation with Clara. It was all very well for him to say that they should renew their efforts and find a way to solve the mystery–but he was damned if he saw how they were going to do it. He sat there, thinking of plans to put to her, and rejecting them all outright as either impossible to carry out, or unlikely to produce results.

I am at a dead end, he thought, regretting immediately the unfortunate choice of words. He had left her in the garden, to go for what he had called "a brief thinking session."

"I'll be back in no time with a plan," he had said optimistically. Now he was facing the prospect of having to tell her that no plan would be forthcoming. This was why he preferred to go on sitting on that bench thinking up plans, even if it took eternity, rather than admit defeat to Clara. Meanwhile, he invested his time in watching a passing snail that seemed to be unable to make up its mind whether to cross the leaf that got in its way, or eat it. He had been at this for quite some time when a dry cough brought him up with a jerk. A man was standing in front of him, gazing at him inquiringly. George gaped at him, recognition coming in a flash. He could hardly believe his eyes, it was his old schoolteacher.

The teacher was looking down to George, in a patronizing manner, just as he had done when he was a fifth grade pupil. In a second he felt like a little boy again. He jumped up, looking for appropriately respectful words of welcome, and finding none.

This man had always had this effect on him. He was a teacher of the old kind, such as you cannot find nowadays. He had started teaching little boys before the war, and held austere views on the respective duties of the pupil and of the Maestro, as they used to call him. *Signor Maestro*, was his title, and nobody would dream of calling him by any other name.

The Maestro carried with him a rare blend of fatherly benevolence and severity. He seldom smiled, and when he did, it was to punctuate praise for a homework well done, or for a beautiful calligraphy. His pupils knew that he was just and inflexible, and the maestro left no doubt that he would administer punishment to the last drop, even though he might be suffering in doing so, even more than they did.

The Maestro had taught him until fifth grade. He never had another teacher like him nor, he believed, had God ever made another teacher to match him. When asked what their feelings were for him, his pupils would invariably say, "Respect."

When the fifth year ended, the Maestro bade farewell to his class. One by one, the pupils filed before him, and each was given a word of advice and farewell, as well as a certificate of attendance to the Maestro's arts class. This was a voluntary-compulsory class, two hours every week, and it was the apple of the Maestro's eyes. It was voluntary, inasmuch as it was extracurricular, and you were not obliged to enroll and attend; and it was compulsory, inasmuch as you did enroll and attend religiously, if you knew what was good for you.

The farewell ceremonies directed by the Maestro were legendary. No two pupils were told the same thing, they said, and most kept his words of farewell as a secret. It was whispered that, when parting from a pupil, the Maestro would tell him exactly his opinion of him. And since the Maestro was infallible in his opinions, the children believed that whatever he told you would rule your future.

The night before the ceremony that marked the end of his fifth year in school, George had barely been able to go to sleep, such was his excitement at the forthcoming event. When sleep finally came, it brought with it an unforgettable dream. In it the Maestro, leaning towards him, told him with a smirk, "You little scoundrel. I am happy to get rid of you, at last. Your handwriting is foul, you can't remember dates, and your diction stinks. You are no good and you will never amount to anything, no matter how much you try. You may as well give up now, since you will always be a failure. Now go away smiling and tell your friends how happy you are."

In the dream, he ran away in tears from the Maestro, toward a chorus of his classmates who were singing cheerfully, "What did he say, young boy? What did he say to you? To you, to youuu! What did he say?"

To which he replied, "He told me something so beautiful that it made me cry."

A scary dream, George had felt at the time.

In reality, when his turn had come, the Maestro had gripped his shoulder and arm, and had murmured into his ear, "I wish I could teach you some more. You are ready for Tomorrow, but you can always come to me for advice. Now go, and don't look back."

The fatherly touch, more than the Maestro's words, had touched George to the point of tears. Later, he had asked a few of his friends about their own send-away from the Maestro.

"Can't tell you," the first one had said.

"C'mon," George had said, "tell me and I'll tell you."

"Well, he has given me a lot of rubbish about being ready for Tomorrow and all that."

"To you too?" said a second boy. "Did he tell you that you can come to him for advice?"

"Yeah," said the first boy, "that too."

"And what did he say to you?" George had been asked.

"Never mind," he had answered. But the magic had been spoiled.

Once, two or three years later, he had nevertheless come to the Maestro for advice. He was having problems with a teacher who disliked him, and no matter what he did, always found him guilty of something. He had tried to seek advice from his father, but midway through his explanation his father started taking the teacher's side, and wouldn't listen any more. He was desperate for support, and had remembered the Maestro's parting words.

He had come to his class one morning, strangely nervous at the thought of meeting him again, and feeling like a fifth-grader once again. There were still a few minutes before the break, and he had peeked in to familiarize himself again with the surroundings. His eyes had met with an old and frail man, his back bent, and his voice weak. The Maestro was instructing a silent class on homework, with a hesitant voice. George had turned back and run away fast, before the Maestro could see him, and had spent the next few days trying to forget what he had seen.

Now, the Maestro stood before him, strong and vital as always.

"Ah, it's you, my boy. I was hoping to see you one of these days. Please sit down. No need, ah, to be formal now. You are a grown man now. Sit, sit. I will sit beside you."

"Maestro—it is so nice to see you. I—"

Words failed him, and he kept looking at his old teacher in disbelief.

"Yes, yes? What were you saying?" the Maestro snorted impatiently.

"I—I missed you. I didn't realize it until now, perhaps, but I did miss you."

"You did, didn't you, ah? Is that why you never sent me a postcard? Ah? Or maybe you were punishing me for teaching you right? Never, ever one postcard, you know? And you never visited me. Ah? All my pupils visited me. All my pupils sent me postcards. But not you. No, sir. Too busy, I suppose?"

"No, no. I left. I moved with my family abroad, and never came back. That's why I never visited you. I would have, I swear. I intended to. You meant a lot to me."

"Well, it is a little late now for apologies, ah? Let's forget about it now. Although I won't tell you I wasn't hurt. I was. But that's beside the point now, ah?"

"But, *Signor Maestro*. What are you doing here? Why didn't you cross the meadow? I am sure you deserve it, and if you don't, then nobody does."

"Why didn't I, you ask? Why didn't I, indeed? Do you remember what I used to tell you in first grade? That you all were my children..."

"–and that you will always look after us, and punish us, as you would have done with your children, had you had any. Yes, I remember that very well. And I remember that you always took good care of us. You made sure that everybody had enough food, and looked after the children that didn't have enough, and shared your food with us. I remember that very well."

"Well, then. What kind of father would I be, I ask you, if I crossed the meadow and left some of my children on this side? What would you think of me, ah? You would say, 'The Maestro teaches well but acts not so well', wouldn't you now? You would say, 'We trusted the Maestro to be here for us, to guide and advise, just as he told us he would be–but no! He has deserted us and gone away'. And you would be right, wouldn't you? Ah?

"No. Many of my children are still here, and some are yet to come. I will go last, as is proper and correct."

"But–"

"No buts. Now tell me why are you still here."

"I am stuck here, because of this dream."

George found it easy to tell him about his dream. In fact, he found it easy to tell him everything. He told him about Clara, and their attempt to discover the truth, and their failure.

"So, you like this girl, what's her name, Clara? Uh?"

"Well, yes. Although I don't know what 'like' means, in this place. I feel sorry for her, and I like her as a person, and I wish I could help, but I don't really know what to do. And perhaps I feel a little guilty, because it's possible that my father had a hand in this–in her being here. And I'm not sure that what we are trying to do is the right thing. Perhaps, if we find out what happened, we will only be sorrier, and still remain stuck on this side. Perhaps it's better not to know. And perhaps there is no way to know."

"Am I hearing you giving up? Never give up! No, sir. You must discover the truth. Knowledge is power. Didn't I teach you that, ah? You must make peace with yourself, before you go. And you can't make peace with something you don't know. But first of all, you must learn a few ground rules of this place."

The Maestro got up and started pacing the ground before the bench.

"Please pay attention," he said curtly, and started to recite.

"Rule number 1, There will be no contacts between yourself and living persons. If you go about making yourself noticed, you may unsettle everybody here. And we can't have that. No.

"Rule number 2, You never question why. It is not your place to argue with any of the tasks that the Divine Providence puts your way while you are here."

"But–"

"Rule number 3–"

"Yes, but I don't understand–"

"*Rule number 3!*" the Maestro continued, raising his voice and eyeing him severely, "Never interrupt your teacher. I thought you knew this rule. You will not interrupt me again, please."

George had not been rebuked for at least thirty years now, and would have rebelled at being treated like a child, had he known how to do it. Instead, he fixed his gaze on the tip of his shoe, and kept quiet as instructed.

"Rule number 4, Cross the meadow as soon as you feel ready. Don't waste time staying behind for unimportant purposes, as you may lose your chance to go.

"If you follow these simple rules, you will get through this place peacefully and safely. Questions?"

George suppressed the urge to raise his hand, and said instead, "I have so many questions, that I don't know where to start. To begin with, who is running this place? Where are we?"

"Well, of course, we are on earth, where else? Where did you think you were? In paradise? Ah–aha," he guffawed. "However, we keep apart from the living persons who inhabit this same place."

"You said 'no contacts with living persons'. But I know that there are certain things that we can do. We can interact with matter. Could you explain this to me?"

"We have very limited possibilities, and no two persons are equally skilled. We can generate sounds that living persons can hear relatively easily–almost everybody can do it. We can project images that living persons can see; images of ourselves or of objects–but that takes a much greater skill than just generating simple sounds. Still, it's a very effective way to manifest ourselves. We can also move small amounts of matter–the amount and type of matter differs from one person to another. This is nothing special, it is just a simple manifestation of telekinesis, you see? Uh?"

"I thought that telekinesis was a power that only a few had."

"In reality, it is a power that everybody has. Everybody. I have it. You have it. You always had it. However, living people lose the ability to use that power at an early age–somewhere between birth and puberty–and it becomes subordinate to earthly routines. Then, when you reach–-uh–our present condition, this, and other powers are liberated and you find it easy to use them. It is that simple, you see?"

"Oh, yes. Very simple." George mused for a while on the explanations of the Maestro. They left him unsatisfied.

"But, *Signor Maestro*, we can also make people act as we wish. We can make them do things. I have done it myself."

"But of course. That is nothing more than rudimentary telepathy. Again, something everybody has, but which is suppressed in the chaotic world in which people live, to the extent that for a living person it becomes mostly a passive sense. You can think of a living person as–uh, a radio receiver. He can receive a telepathic transmission, and he could have kept the power to generate one, had he taken the trouble to exercise his telepathic powers as a child. Since he normally has not exercised, he cannot transmit, but only receives on a very elementary level. Very simple. You see, normal people suppress such powers at an early stage, because they don't need them, and because they instinctively sense that exercising them would make them different from everybody else. It is the instinct of the herd, to be 'normal' you must give up powers that have been given to you. But we, in–uh, our condition–we can't move around without those minimal powers."

"Then how come I can't transmit or receive from you?"

"But, for heaven's sake, my boy. What do you think we are

doing right now? Talking? Ah?"

He had never thought until then about the nature of their communication. The look on his face gave him away, and the Maestro let out a hearty laugh and went on.

"You did think we were talking! Didn't you? Didn't you? Aha! You did!"

This was the first time the George had ever heard the Maestro laugh openly, and he was not enjoying it. Most offensive, the Maestro was being, he thought.

"It felt like talking," he said accusingly. "How would I know any different?"

"Common sense, my boy. Use your common sense. The world is overcrowded with people in–uh–our condition. Imagine every one of us actually talking! The living people would not be able to hear themselves thinking. So it must be something living persons cannot hear. Common sense, that's all it takes, you see."

"I guess there is much more for me to learn here," he said. "Meanwhile, I don't really know what to do next."

"But, of course, you must go and solve that little mystery of yours, together with that nice young lady of whom you were speaking."

"Well, Maestro, it is easier said than done. There is very little that we ourselves can do, and we need the help of living people, which we can't get."

"Yes, you can. Not only you can, but you must also get some help from a living person, and I think I know the one. But remember, you're not allowed to contact him directly in any way. Come, I'll show you what to do." Having said that, the Maestro started walking away, without turning back to see if he was following.

There was no question about it. The Maestro had issued his order, and George had to follow. I am so weak, he thought with shame, that I can be ordered about even after my death. Resigned, he followed in the Maestro's footstep, with a bowed head and eyes fixed on the ground before him.

CHAPTER XIII
David

David was tired. He had just arrived home from a long day at the university, where he taught a course in Applied History. As to what Applied History was, most of his colleagues at the university were not quite clear. It had to do with crime, and old crime at that, but nobody really bothered to understand what the syllabus really meant, and that was all right by David, who hated to hear criticism from his colleagues, even if it was served under the title of "constructive suggestions." He had a very high opinion of himself, and felt that everybody else was professionally way below him.

Born in London thirty-seven years before, David had been drawn towards the study of crime since he first read about Jack the Ripper. As a teenager he had often dreamt of solving the mystery and unveiling his identity–a project long since abandoned. At the age where everything seems possible, he had roamed the ill-famed streets where the murders had taken place, as if the walls could tell him the story. He liked the feeling of the street at night, particularly when it was damp, when water drizzles materialize out of the mist, and small moist needles hit your face and hands. He was not afraid of the dark, and he liked to linger in spots where he imagined that a murderer might be lurking in wait for a fair young lady returning home alone. He imagined himself in the role of rescuer, rushing to the aid of the victim-to-be. He used to run the imaginary sequence of events in his mind, frame by frame, until it became real to him, down to the smallest detail. Then he would wonder whether this was what had really happened in one of those alleys, more than a century ago. Perhaps these walls could tell him their secrets. And perhaps that was what they were doing, he sometimes fantasized. Maybe these images in his mind were not pure imagination, but rather a re-run of something that had really happened, an event that had left its impression on those walls, and they were now projecting it back to him.

With the passing of the years he had outgrown these childish fantasies, and had shaped himself into a hard-lined scientist. Working at the faculty of criminology as a mere research assistant, he had attained some degree of fame when, while preparing a report on high suicide-rate neighborhoods, he had stumbled upon the discovery of a serial killer who had been cleverly disguising his murders as disappearances and suicides. Moreover, he had done so only by reading written police reports of the isolated cases, and finding hints of a connection between them.

He showed quite a knack at discovering incongruous details, and had been called upon on a number of occasions to assist the police in the analysis of data too bulky for them. Although no other major success had come his way, he had been reasonably useful in a few investigations, and had thus gained the respect of investigative circles.

His present position as a university professor had been offered to him five years earlier, and he had gladly accepted it, although this meant leaving his homeland. David's decision had been influenced by the lavish research fund that went with the job. It was a new university chair, sponsored by a French historian who had made millions by the simple methodology of waiting for his wife's wealthy relatives, and then his wife, to die before him. He had always been a thoroughly unsuccessful historian who never developed a theory, or managed to shed light on any historical period. He had nevertheless found that money can cure ineptness, at least if you are willing to spend enough of it. He had thus gone around Europe, finding universities willing to accept good money and, in return, dedicate grants, projects, and buildings to his name. These universities would turn a blind eye on the embellished biography of their generous donor, and were willing to let him speak at dedication ceremonies, for as long as his money warranted it. His donations increased as time passed, as if he were afraid that his self-powered memorial program might be running out of time.

After a while Monsieur Lavoix, the French donor, had decided that his lifelong contribution to "Applied History"—by which he meant the use of history for useful purposes—had to be passed on to posterity. The fact that he had coined the term a few days before, and that he had never done any work on the subject, did not seem to discourage him. His "friends" were unable to believe that he would ever have an original idea, and it was thus whispered in university circles that the old bore had gotten the notion from reading science fiction comics. This was how David's research fund and cathedra were created; and the money being put in by Monsieur Lavoix was quite generous.

The interview between Monsieur Lavoix and David had been a short one. It had all started on the day when the Dean of his faculty had summoned David with urgency. This Dean, David knew, had come to dislike him intensely over the years, almost as much as the faculty did. There were many reasons for this dislike: his manners were not in line with what the university preferred; he was outspoken, did not show proper respect to his superiors, and was generally a pain in the neck to one and all. Above all, however, he had "A Record"–he had accomplished a substantial practical success in a very early stage of his career, which was viewed with concern in academic circles as demeaning to the institution. The academy, most scholars maintained, had the sacred duty to pursue Knowledge. Putting Knowledge to a practical end, they felt, was a common and plebeian thing to do. What David had done was therefore unheard of, and had left many a professor aghast.

"If this thing spreads," one influential professor of little known Mesopotamian languages had complained to the Dean, "they may start demanding that we make ourselves useful."

"This is very dangerous indeed," the Dean had agreed gravely. "We can't have that here. Something must be done about it. We must think. We must think."

Still, political undercurrents at the university did not easily permit a way to get rid of David, because of his academic reputation. On the other hand, tenure was not a topic of conversation where David was concerned.

It was thus with some trepidation that David received the summons from the Dean. He had gotten along reasonably well with him over the years, or at least so he thought, but there had never been such an urgent call for his company in the middle of the day, and the secretary who had called him could not–or would not–provide any hint as to its reasons. The Dean was waiting for him impatiently, pacing the room.

"Hello, David. Come in, come in, come in," he had said cheerfully, when David had rapped on the door. "I have a jolly good surprise for you. How would you like to get yourself a nice cathedra in Applied History?"

"Well, it depends."

"It depends on what?"

"First of all, on what 'Applied History' means, if anything."

"What on earth does that have to do with my question?" the Dean had asked peevishly. "How many people do you think really do work that is connected with their cathedra?"

"Almost nobody, I guess."

"Correct. That is not how you plan an academic career. The way you go about it is that first of all you get your own cathedra, and *then* you decide what you want to do with it. The only tricky part is to find a good enough semantic connection between the name of the cathedra and work that you actually do. That's why a cathedra in 'Applied History' is so valuable. You can use the funds to research engineering principles of the Babylonians, or the healing leaves of Black Africa, and no questions asked. So what it really boils down to is, do you want a cathedra, or don't you?"

"Well, if you put it like that, I definitely do. I can see no downside to it. Which faculty is going to host it? History?

Criminology?"

"Not precisely."

"Egyptology? Seismology?" He had suddenly stopped, perceiving that something was wrong. "Wait a minute. Where is the catch?"

"No catch. Honestly. However, the cathedra is not going to be hosted by our university. The benefactor, who is going to donate the money for it, insists on its being located on the continent. This benefactor is a Frenchman, you know," the Dean had said, lowering his voice conspiratorially, "and you must make allowances. Besides, he donates quite a lot to our faculty, and we cannot alienate him by refusing to make the recommendation he requested."

"So why me?" David had asked, suspiciously.

"He has come over to England, head hunting, and we have been asked to make a recommendation. And of course your name has come up immediately, as everybody here at the faculty holds you in high esteem and feels you are a most deserving chap."

This was, in truth, a somewhat tamed report of the facts. What had really happened was that the request for a recommendation had been discussed at a faculty meeting. At the meeting the view had been unanimous that this was, as someone quite neatly put it, "a most admirable opportunity to get rid of that appalling chap, David what's-his-name." A vote had been quickly taken to recommend him for the position, and a silent prayer had been offered by many a professor, that David might indeed be the chosen one.

"Well, I appreciate your confidence," said David, mollified. "I would definitely like to have a stab at it. Ha, ha–" David laughed at his own joke, "seeing that I am in the middle of a comparative work on 'The Most Notorious Knife Killers'."

"Ha, ha," the Dean had concurred dryly.

"So what do I do next?"

"The benefactor–Monsieur Lavoix, would like you to join him for dinner at the Grill Room of the Savoy. Please be there at seven p.m. on the dot, as he will be waiting for you, and I am told that he values punctuality."

"I will, I will," David had said, adding as an afterthought "I don't know how to thank you. I appreciate this opportunity very much."

"Don't thank me. Thank yourself. You deserve it. You certainly deserve it. I look forward to hearing that you have been chosen for this cathedra. Don't fail us. The honor of this faculty is in your hands. Now I suggest that you go and prepare yourself," he added, concluding the discussion. "He will certainly ask you questions on your views of Applied History, and I think that you should take some time now to review the background."

That is how, on that same day, David had found himself at six p.m. pacing feverishly in front of the Savoy. He was not going to take a chance and be late. At five minutes to seven he had reached the Grill Room, where the Maitre d' had directed him to his host's table.

Monsieur Lavoix was short and stocky, and wore a tie that would have elicited comment even in Paris.

"Welcome, my young friend," he had said genially, getting up to greet David. "Please sit down and have *en peu de champagne*. I am happy that you could join me tonight. Please tell me something about yourself. About yourself, and also about you," he had added, somewhat cryptically.

David had done his best to appear, at the same time, intelligent, serious, enchanting, secure, malleable, strong, earnest, and friendly, while touching only on neutral topics. The conversation had somewhat been hampered by the fact that Monsieur Lavoix appeared to speak only a very rudimentary–and often unintelligible–brand of English. He did seem to be perfectly at ease, however, and entirely unaware of his linguistic limitations. After a few minutes of aimless conversation, he had gone straight to the point.

"Mr. David, my friend, I hear you are spoken very well here in *Angleterre*. What I need is someone who can implement my theories. No doubt you have heard of my theories on *l'application de l'histoire?*" David had nodded frantically, although, in spite of his efforts throughout that afternoon, he had not been able to find a single serious article or book that mentioned his host's name.

"So if I establish your cathedra for you, I thank you for developing my theories and making the research of it at all times. Particularly, *l'application* of the global theory to the renewed analysis of basic history–this is very close to my heart. This is the essence of my request. So now, Monsieur David, are you or don't you not?"

David had no idea whatsoever of what his benefactor-to-be was talking about, but answered without blushing.

"Monsieur Lavoix. Let me tell you this. I assure you that if you choose to entrust me with your cathedra, I will consider it a sacred honor to perpetuate your work and to highlight your contribution to Applied History."

"I knew that you were the right person. I knew it! You

came to me so highly recommended that it could not be otherwise. Can you leave on Sunday?"

This is why David, in deference to his French sponsor, was now involved in the study of murders carried out during the French revolution, disguised as executions of nobility. He liked his work very much, and when he indulged in introspection, which was seldom, always concluded that he was moderately happy. He had a few friends with whom he sporadically had a good time, and every now and then he sought feminine company, although his interest in women was tepid at most.

He could not see the two figures standing beside him.

"This is the person, my boy," said the Maestro. "He is the one who can do something for you. However, you must make him take an interest in your case, and that's your task. You will do it delicately, ah? No use rushing him. He is busy with other things, and must be guided very carefully, otherwise he will never pick up your problem."

"Who is he?" asked George.

"He is a professor of Applied History–a–uh–somewhat unknown branch of criminology. You might think of him as a time detective. He–uh–solves old mysteries, and the older the better. He is quite a bright person, when he puts himself to a task. Quite capable, quite capable indeed."

"Yes, but how–"

The maestro held up a hand in a silencing motion.

"That's your problem, my boy. I can't help there. Ask your girl to help. Study him closely before you do anything, ah?"

"Can't you help more, Maestro?"

"Haven't I done enough already?"

"Well, I don't know," George answered, looking at David

with a critical eye. "I'm not sure that he can do anything, or if he can, that he will want to. This possible murder, it's not something really interesting, no famous people are involved. He may think it not worth his while."

"That is indeed a problem, my boy. I hope you can solve it."

"But what if I can't? What if I can't find a way to make him investigate? I don't know what to do." He started to despair at the thought of the obstacles that had to be surmounted. "I can't very well talk to the man, for God's sake!"

"Don't start swearing now. You make me ashamed of you. Of course you can find a way. And if you don't, well, I don't know."

"Maestro, how can I find you if I need advice on this?"

"If I can make time, I will come to you, but I guess that I will be pretty busy elsewhere. I have many other pupils, you know. And their problems are heavy and real, not petty problems like your dream. Tcha! A man of your age indulging in dreams of this kind, I ask you. Bah!"

"But, Maestro, for me it is a big–"

"Well," the Maestro said cheerfully, "I'll be gone now. Be careful. Be *very* careful."

"Careful about what?" he asked, suddenly worried lest unknown dangers may lie ahead.

But with these last words of admonition, the Maestro turned on his heels, and was gone. George realized that he had been rebuked, again. And through no fault of his own too, just as in school when somebody else used to throw paper darts and the Maestro would always pick him to blame. There were a hundred things he might have told the Maestro; repartees that would have shown him he was no longer the spineless child he had known in school; witty retorts that would have shown him that he was no longer in charge. Unfortunately, none of this had occurred to him before the Maestro disappeared, and he had no idea how to find him. What's more, he was not sure that he ever wanted to see that old pompous schoolteacher again.

George turned to study David. What he saw was a man not more than forty, well looking, flat-bellied and in good shape. His apartment was cluttered with books, files, and paper of every type, color, and shape. Much of it was scattered about the shelves or on the carpet. David had a cleaning woman coming in twice a week, but she was under strict instructions to leave paper alone. She was allowed to deal with everything else at her discretion, but no piece of paper was to be moved one tenth of an inch from its usual place.

George realized there was no woman around here. A woman would never have permitted such a chaotic, cozy atmosphere. This was definitely a bachelor's house. It was neat, though, and hauntingly so. No dirty plate in the sink, or any half-emptied glass around the house. It was, in a word...neat. He hoped the Maestro hadn't found him a gay investigator. Not that there was anything wrong with it, he added hastily to himself—a line he had heard somewhere on television, and which always seemed able to put bad sentences right.

CHAPTER XIV
Building an Interest

The book was not developing as planned. Some of the threads leading to the Rochat family, apparently murdered for gold by fake revolutionaries, had reached a dead end. David was annoyed. This line of investigation had seemed very promising at first, but was now drying up. The Rochats, it seemed, were merchants that had reached some economic eminence in Paris. The head of the family, Jean-Paul Rochat, was a supplier of fine linen, spices and other goods used predominantly by the aristocracy, and had thus developed strong relations with the King's court. For many years, Jean-Paul Rochat had applied all his economic influence in a vain attempt to convince the King to bestow upon him a title that would make him a nobleman, and thus permit him to join that aristocracy he admired and envied so much. Those who heard this preposterous idea from him laughed secretly at the thought that a merchant could become a nobleman. One of the King's closest consultants, a viscount, had been quoted as saying that "the day this shopkeeper will go around with a title will mark the end of the kingdom." He little knew how right he had been.

The French Revolution began, and with it the disintegration of the aristocracy. During the last days of the kingdom, Jean-Paul Rochat decided to seize the opportunity and try to achieve his life-long goal. Armed with gold and other valuables, he had gone to Versailles and knocked on the gates. A viscount (maybe the very same one who had sneered at Rochat's ambitions), who was about to flee the palace, took time off to sell him a fake document with the royal seal, which made him a Count. Word got around quickly in those days and, returning home from the palace, he was captured together with his family by a band of brigands posing as revolutionaries, and was murdered. His shop and home were taken over by the brigands' families, who flourished running them, and lived happily ever after.

David had relied heavily on this family and on the tale of vanity that went with it, to carry the bulk of the narrative in his book, and had practically made it the core of his work, only to discover that they were dying on him too soon to make good material for more than one chapter. His irritation at the need to re-think the whole set-up was therefore considerable. Still, he had enough material to write the next chapter. He had been debating whether to leave the city for the weekend or to work through it, but the weather forecast, promising mostly uninterrupted rain, had decided for him. The one pastime of his youth to which he had remained addicted was horse riding. It was incredibly difficult to find a decent horse near a big city on the continent, and he had had to make do with horses of inferior level. He had never been reticent about his views of the quality of his mounts, and this had cost him the only good horse he had been able to find since leaving England. It happened on a day when, coming to ride at the appointed time, he was handed a horse that, at first sight, clearly appeared not to be up to his standards.

"What is this?" he inquired.

"It's a horse, sir," answered the stable owner.

"Where is my regular horse?"

"It's resting. The vet has given it a shot on account of a swelling it has developed."

"Well, then bring me a decent replacement."

"This is a very good animal."

"I am not talking about his disposition. I am sure it is amiable, if it ever wakes up. But this is a lame mule, and I do not intend to ride it."

"This is the best horse I have."

The proprietor started to show signs of impatience, but David went on unheedingly.

"Well, my dear man, if this is the best horse you can produce, I am sure that your stable is in trouble. In bad trouble. I am not stupid enough, I think, to take this miserable beast that you try to pass for a horse, instead of my regular mount. I insist on getting my regular horse, or a mount to match it, and I won't take a joke like this so-called horse instead. I believe that I am entitled to service, seeing that it was early last week that I reserved my horse for today. And let me tell you that I give little credit to your story on the ailment of my horse. I find it thin. I assume that you have given it to somebody else and now you are trying to cover for it. Well, then?"

Throughout this tirade the stable owner had stood scowling silently at him. Now he took the cigarette on which he had been chewing out of his mouth, and addressed David with a smile.

"Are you finished?"

"Not quite, I–"

"Because if you don't get into your car in under thirty seconds, and get the hell off my land," he continued, still smiling, "I shall break your leg, got it?"

"I–"

"And if you ever show your ugly face again here, I shall break your leg *and* your arm, okay?"

David had seldom received a clearer and more unambiguous explanation that left no doubt as to the options open to him. The proprietor serenely opened the door of David's car and gestured him in, and David, still dazed by his reaction, got into the car without a word.

"Have a nice day," said the proprietor, slamming the door after him.

It had taken David quite a while to brace himself to find a new stable—in an altogether different area, where the proprietor was unlikely to know his former stable owner—and he had learnt to come to terms with the quality of the horses that were offered him, without complaining. He liked riding too much to give it up. But in this weather, riding was out of the question.

He was now at his computer, working on the first page of his chapter, which he had unimaginatively titled, "Murder of the Rochat family."

The Rochat family lived in Paris, he wrote, *and owned a number of shops that sold fine and expensive goods.*

He looked at what he had just written, and thought it was the worst beginning, ever, to a chapter. He stopped typing and studied the page, looking for inspiration. The title read, *Where is Clara F.?*

He wondered where on earth that had come from. He hadn't written it, so maybe it had been left in the computer's memory from some other document, although he could recall none with that name.

David didn't like computers. To him they were a sad necessity, but he had never come to understand them. He'd had a hard time learning to use one, and it was his secret belief that computers always did their best to trouble him, deleting files he needed, and printing out garbled text when he was in a hurry.

He deleted the unwelcome words, and painstakingly retyped the title, so that it now read "Murder of the Rochat family."

Or so he thought.

The title read, *Has Clara Fini been murdered?*

David felt a chill running along his spine. Was he going mad?

He thought that someone must have been playing tricks on him. Suddenly, the only rational explanation came to him, It must be Mario. I'll kill him.

Mario, his colleague at the university, was a computer wizard. He had been at David's house last week, to help him fix a problem apparently created by a virus that had found its way into his PC. He had explained to David at great length about 'macros' and other entities of names that, to him, sounded equally insignificant. Mario was fond of his computers, and was excited at the opportunity to explain about them to David, and to indoctrinate him into learning to love them.

"Computers are good," he had said. "You should learn to exploit them."

"I have no desire to get acquainted with this foul machine, beyond my basic need to use it as a typewriter," was David's answer.

"A computer is not a typewriter," Mario had argued.

"Well, it is for me. I wish it could fulfill at least this one simple function right. Apparently, that is asking for too much."

"A PC is a versatile machine. It can perform an infinite number of tasks. It can be used as a communication device, or to create paintings, or to make music. It is definitely not a typewriter. And because of its complexity, it sometimes suffers from problems, like the one we have here now, which was caused by a computer virus. That is the price you pay to have such a wonderful machine in your hands."

"But I don't want it to perform an infinite number of tasks. I want it to behave itself and be a good typewriter. And not to break down every other day. Is that too much to ask?"

"Tell me, do you surf the web?"

"Do I what to which?"

"The Internet. Surely even you have heard of the Internet."

"Of course I have. Very useful thing for research."

"Well, then."

"Well then what?"

"You couldn't get on the Internet without the complicated and sophisticated processes that are carried out by your computer."

"You don't know what you're talking about. It may be complicated in your PC, but in mine, all I have to do is click this little thingy here–you see," he had added, pointing at an icon on the screen, "and in no time I am on the Internet. Very simple. A child could do it. Maybe you should get a new PC."

"You really don't know anything about computers, do you? Let me explain a few basic facts to you."

Mario had embarked upon a long and detailed explanation of the basics of computer science. David had politely posed as listening, but had not heard a word of what he had said (nor would he have understood it if he had), except that you can make wonderful things happen to your computer programs, if you write the right macros for it.

Now Mario's explanations came back to him. He was a bit sketchy on the details of what Mario had told him, but he was pretty sure that the main thrust of it was that you can make a PC do virtually everything, if you know how to program it.

The solution to the whole mystery was now evident. It was obvious that this must be Mario's way to be funny, and to teach him at the same time.

He picked up the phone and dialed Mario's home number, hoping that he had not gone away for the weekend. The phone was picked up almost immediately.

"Yes," a sleepy voice mumbled.

"Is that you, Mario?"

"Yes. Do you know what time is it?"

"Just a little after midnight. Listen–"

"No, you listen. It is two a.m. I am asleep, and I plan to go on doing it. Call me tomorrow."

"This is important, Mario. It's about that macro that you planted in my PC," said David, playing the old I-know-what-you-did-and-there-is-no-point-in-denying-it trick.

"I don't know what you are talking about." Mario's voice was at once attentive and puzzled. "I wrote no macros for your computer."

"Then tell me why is it behaving in a funny way?"

"Qualify 'funny'."

"Writing things of its own accord."

"David, have you been drinking?"

"No, I haven't been drinking," David answered peevishly. "I am trying to get some work done, and the damn machine keeps getting in the way."

"Explain in full," Mario said, in a resigned tone.

David explained his recent experience, voicing an opinion that it was indeed "funny."

"Well, I don't know what caused it, but it wasn't me," said Mario. "I did nothing at all to your computer, save fix it. It's probably your imagination playing tricks on you. Go and get some sleep and it'll go away. Good night." He hung up.

"Good night," answered David, to a dead receiver. Mario's plea of innocence had seemed genuine enough. So it wasn't him. And he was the only one who had got near his computer. And at the moment he could think no other explanation.

On an impulse, he got up and went to the telephone directory. He found twenty-seven entries for "Fini" in the book. He read through them, but none of them was a "Clara Fini." Maybe she didn't exist at all. Or perhaps she did, but was unlisted, or was the child of someone in the directory; or maybe she lived in another city. Or perhaps, if she had died, she was no longer in the book. The possibilities were too many, and it was better to forget all about it. He knew it would probably all look stupid in the morning, anyway.

All of a sudden he felt wasted. He went to the kitchen to fix himself a cup of tea, undressed quickly, and went to bed, resolved not to think about this strange occurrence any more. He got into bed and closed his eyes, and was soon floating away. He hadn't realized until now how tired he was, after a whole week of teaching, writing and researching. He deserved a good night's sleep.

He let himself drift into that blessed state where you know that you will soon be asleep, and where, for a brief moment, you don't have a care in the world. The blanket of sleep was closing over him, and he was surprised to hear a voice whispering in his right ear, "Find Clara," and another, more distant voice, echoing, "Where is she?" He tried to open his eyes, uncertain of the origin of these voices, and struggled to wake up, but he was already asleep.

"So your surname is Fini?"

"As if you didn't know. We have been introduced before."

"You are right. But I had forgotten all about it. I told you so. Sometimes I think that I have forgotten most of my childhood, and that what I recall is only a figment of my imagination, something that I have made up to fill in the voids. Perhaps I remember things that I would have liked to have happened. And maybe my dream is also nothing more than imagination."

"I don't think so. You may have made up nice memories, but I don't see you inventing spooky ones."

"Why didn't you tell me your surname before?"

"We don't use family names much over here. They don't

mean anything anymore. Besides, I thought you knew it, Giorgio."

"It's George now. Or rather was. But you're right, it doesn't matter any more. We know who we are, and we know each other."

"Right. No more phone bills to pay, no formal papers to fill in. Names don't count any more. Except that your friend David must learn to know my name very well."

"We'll be after him until he is so curious about you that he will have no choice but to investigate."

"Do you think it'll work?"

"I honestly don't know. But this David is our only option right now. He investigates old mysteries for a living, and he is probably the only one we can get to take an interest in our case. Provided there is a case, that is. We must start him on the right track, but we must be careful because, if he can't find anything, he will cool off."

"I'm sure there is something for him to investigate. I am certainly more recent than this Rochelle family of his."

"Rochat," he corrected her. "Don't start being jealous now," he admonished her. "You barely know the guy."

"I'm not jealous. I only think that I deserve more attention than an obscure French Revolution family."

"You deserve a lot of attention. But you can't blame him so far. He doesn't know that you exist."

"Although I've made myself noticeable to him tonight, haven't I?"

"Yeah. Definitely. You know, I thought that the trick with the computer was rather neat."

"Well, it's simpler than those things you did on the tram.

All it involves is to make him hit the key you want, instead of that which he was planning to hit. It is a kind of high-tech Ouija Board."

"What is a Ouija Board?"

"It's a board with letters and numbers written on it. You turn a cup upside down and everybody puts its finger on the top of it. Then you push it around and make it stop on a letter, and you read out words from the succession of letters. It's very simple. But the keyboard is a much simpler and quicker way to do it."

"I see now. We are using him as a vehicle of communication between us."

"As long as he doesn't realize what's going on, and doesn't resist, we can make him do it. But if he understands what's happening, he can stop it, and then we lose our best channel of communication. We must be very careful not to overdo it. It was the same with the Ouija Board with which we used to play when I was a child. Once one of the players decided to influence the game, or became scared or skeptical, we had to ask him to remove his finger, since otherwise nothing more would come out of the board."

"Well, let's go now."

"Don't you think that we should stick around for a while longer?"

"I see no point. There's nothing more we can do for tonight anyway. He looks like someone who is not going to come around for twelve hours."

In fact, David got up after eight hours sleep, refreshed. The strange occurrence of last night had faded away, and was no long bothering him. It is true that it had had an effect on him, to the point of making him dream of voices, but it was morning now, and it was all gone. He resolved to forget all about it. Well, maybe he would take a look through the archives, to see if the name Clara Fini added up to anything, but only when he had time. Probably not in the next two months anyway, since he was too busy now working on his book. Sometime in the future, he promised himself. He must make a note not to forget.

He didn't know it, but he was not going to be allowed to forget.

CHAPTER XV
Finding Clues

Maria liked to get up late. She usually worked the afternoon shift at the pharmacy, so as to be able to see the twins off to school, and also linger in bed with her coffee and newspapers. She was not only lazy. She also had an arrangement with the janitor of their building, a young and good-looking man, who would come up to her apartment in the late mornings, and fix an occasional problem with the electric system or the plumbing, when he was not too busy sleeping with her. He had two great qualities, at least from Maria's point of view, he combined a docile nature with a level of intelligence only slightly above that of a retarded child. He could be ordered about, and didn't mind it. And he had no scruples about getting paid by Maria for repair work that went beyond his duties as a janitor, regardless of having had sex with her only a few minutes before. Their arrangement was convenient for both of them, and they never talked about it openly. He accepted the sex with Maria just as he accepted the tea and cookies that the old lady on the second floor offered him when she called on him to fix a window that would not open, or a leaky pipe. To his simple mind these were nothing more than privileges that went with the job, and he never tried to read any significance into his relationship with Maria.

This morning he was taking apart the hot water system. Maria had been hearing noises from the pipes at the back of her bedroom for a week now, and had become convinced that something was seriously wrong with them. It had started on a Friday night, when she had woken up at the sound of Berto's voice calling to her from the bathroom–or so she thought. She had gone to the bathroom and turned on the light, annoyed that Berto would be so miserly as not to turn on the lights even when he had to pee in the middle of the night; and wondering why, if he had to go to the bathroom, he had to wake her up too. But Berto was not there (he was in the dining room, adding up figures for last month's expenses) and the bathroom was empty. A strange gurgling sound had been coming from the pipe that led to the tub. She suddenly remembered that the tap had leaked and wetted the floor only a few days before. She put her ear to the pipes, trying to locate the origin of the noise.

"*Gurgh-shhhh,*" went the pipe. The noise seemed to be coming from the middle of the bathroom, far away from its origin, as she knew that sounds would do in silent and empty houses. But when she moved to the center of the bathroom, there was the noise again, coming from the bathtub.

"*Clang– Gurgh-shhhh* " it went.

She turned the tap, letting out a little water, and the light went off. She had not heard the light switch click, and she turned to see who had done so, half expecting to see Berto in the doorway. But there was nobody there, and the corridor was silent.

"Berto," she called, in sudden panic.

"Yes, honey," his distant voice answered from the dining room.

She almost ran into the dining room, relieved to see his familiar figure in the sparingly lit room.

"Something is terribly wrong with the water pipes," she said. "I thought I heard you calling and I went to the bathroom. The pipes make terrible hissing noises. And while I was checking it out, the lights went off. Do you think that water may have leaked into the electrical system?"

"I don't think so," Berto said with a smile. "I took a bath not so long ago, and there were no noises of any kind, and the lights were fine. You are just imagining things."

"Oh, I don't know," Maria said, unconvinced. A sudden thought occurred to her, "Why are you working at this time of the night?"

"I'm just balancing the figures for last month's expenses. I can hardly find time for it during the day nowadays, with all the pressure of work at the hospital. And I am afraid that we have quite exceeded our budget."

"I don't want to hear about it now. Do you know what time it is?"

"You are right, it is late. I should call it a day."

"Are you sure you were not calling to me? It sounded just like you."

"You were probably dreaming. I haven't moved from here."

"Well, anyway, I think something is wrong with the water pipes. We should call a plumber and have him check the whole system."

"You know very well that we can't afford to replace the plumbing right now. Look at these figures here."

"I\m not going to look at any figures," she said malevolently. "I am going back to bed."

"But, honey–"

"Hey, what is that clanging noise?"

"It sounds like someone hitting a pipe with something."

"You see? I told you I wasn't dreaming. You will wait until the plumbing blows up and drowns us in our sleep before you do anything, won't you?"

"You know that nothing dangerous can really happen. At most, we will have a leaky pipe and we'll deal with it, if and when."

"Have it your own way, but mark my words, we are courting trouble by ignoring that noise. Now I'm going to bed, seeing that there is no point talking sense to you."

She had gone back to bed, piqued. She was too tired to pick a real fight.

Since then, she had been woken up almost every night, for one reason or another, by different noises filtering through her bedroom door, or by one of the twins who did not know any better than to shake her awake to tell her that there were noises in the bathroom. As if she didn't know that already.

A plumber called surreptitiously by Maria during the day had pronounced the plumbing decrepit and badly in need of replacement, but intact and not leaking anywhere.

"You can expect it to start leaking everywhere soon,

though," he had added in a hopeful manner, "and I would redo the whole thing if I were you. Very bad thing a pipe leaking under the floor, that is. And hot water, it's the worst, you know. Much worse than cold water."

"Yes, thank you. I will discuss this with my husband and we will certainly call you soon to do the job."

"And you know what else, ma'am?" he had volunteered, "I would have that heating system checked, if I were you. It looks old to me, and if gas starts to leak—well, that's another ball game altogether."

"Do you think it may be dangerous?"

"Well, I don't want to alarm you, but I was reading in the paper the other day 'bout this whole family that got exterminated by not paying enough attention to the gas system. They were all killed in their sleep, you know. 'Asphyxiated' the paper said, the father of the family, the mother, the little baby they had in the cradle, the elder boy, the young girl, the—"

"Yes, yes. I understand. You have made your point, thank you."

"And I think it was the same make of gas boiler as you have here," he continued helpfully. "You don't see many of them around now, 'cause they are pretty old. I would have that system checked, if I were you," he had concluded, and had left, satisfied at the display of knowledgeable and unbiased service he had given to his perspective client.

The moment the plumber had left, she had called upon the janitor and demanded a full and thorough inspection of the heating system. He was now trying to dismantle the outer casing of the gas boiler, sweating profusely in the process.

"They haven't inspected the heating system for decades,

you know," the janitor said.

He was fumbling with the handle of a small door that was partly hidden behind the gas water boiler. The handle would not turn and he was afraid to break it. A small flame always burned in the boiler, to ensure that no gas would escape into the apartment. Nevertheless, for quite some time now, Maria had been nurturing the notion that it would kill them one day, and the plumber's gruesome report had caused all her hidden fears to surface. But her husband would not budge.

"We will wake up dead one day, because of this gas you insist in keeping in the house", she had told Berto countless times, and again last night, in the worst argument they had had in years. Nevertheless, a new boiler was out of the question. They had no money in their budget for this kind of extravagance. Besides, he had argued with her, everybody has used gas boilers for two hundred years, and they are very safe. "Not this one," she had said, but to no avail. Now, she secretly hoped, this noise perhaps meant that the old boiler was dead and would have to be replaced, whether Berto liked it or not.

At the other end of the small bathroom Clara and George were watching the janitor's work.

"I hope that the box is still there," Clara said.

"I hope so too. It has been hard work to make all those noises. What exactly *is* in the box?"

"I told you. When I left home to come to stay with your father, I brought with me a few personal things that I didn't want to leave behind. Fake jewelry, a couple of photographs of myself with a friend and with my first boyfriend, a school distinction award."

"Distinction award! I didn't know that you liked to study."

"Oh, I did. I was very good in elementary school, but I had to drop out eventually, because my family had no money for that."

"And why did you put it behind that boiler?"

"It seemed like a good idea at the time. There was some personal stuff in it I didn't want your father to see, so I hid it. I wasn't planning to leave it there for so long, of course. It was supposed to be a temporary hiding place, but I never got a chance to retrieve it. Look!" she cried.

The janitor had at last succeeded in opening the lid of the receptacle behind which the hot water and the gas pipes were hidden. He was taking out a small red box.

"Look here, Maria. This was inside. Do you know anything about it?"

"I have never seen it. Let me look at it."

The box was made of cardboard covered by red silk. Golden dragons decorated its lid. The fabric was in a bad state, partly covered with mold, and stained by humidity. It felt damp, and it was heavy. Maria took it aside to the sink, and tried to open it. A small padlock kept it closed. A pathetic little lock kept two small rings together. Maria shook it lightly, and the rings, no longer holding their grip in the damp cardboard, gave way. She opened it and saw a photograph. It was a photograph of a young woman, a girl in fact, and a very beautiful one. Beneath the photograph a few trinkets rested beside a small stack of letters, held together by a pink ribbon. And below them she saw what seemed to be a school certificate.

"It's all still there, just as I remembered it," Clara said, looking over Maria's shoulder.

"Let's see what she does with it."

Maria closed the lid, and put the box under her arm.

"There is nothing of value here, but I'll take a look later," she said to the janitor. "It seems like something that some girl who lived here before us might have hidden and forgotten. I guess I should find who she was and return it to her."

"Hey! Look at these pipes here," cried the janitor, his attention having turned back to the gas boiler. "They are all eroded, and it's a miracle that this boiler hasn't blown up already. You must have it replaced immediately, and in the meantime, you shouldn't use it. It's really dangerous."

"I'll talk to Berto as soon as he gets back. Thanks."

"I can turn the gas off at the mains, to make sure that there is no danger, but that will leave you with no hot water."

"Never mind. I don't want to wake up dead on account of the gas. Turn it off."

"There you go," the janitor said, having firmly turned off the main gas inlet. He seemed satisfied with his work, as if he had performed some particularly difficult deed.

He looked at Maria, expecting some other, more intimate expressions of gratitude. George, who was watching him from the side, thought that he reminded him of a dog he had a few years back. It was a stupid dog, and every time it made its daily excretions stood still and awaited a pat on the head. He would not move without being patted, and George had to pat him in spite of his dislike for the procedure. The janitor was looking just like that dog, when he stood still waiting for its pat on the head. Maria was too curious about the contents of the box, though, to be concerned with other matters.

"I'll go and get some rest now. Thank you," Maria said in a dismissive way.

The janitor's jaw dropped, making him look like a dog that had unexpectedly been kicked.

"Isn't he something?" Clara asked. During the last few days they had become well acquainted with the janitor, and with Maria's escapades with him. "I don't know who of the two is the more despicable."

"I didn't know you were a puritan," George said jokingly.

"Given my profession, you mean," Clara joked back.

"I didn't mean anything," George said, defensively.

"You'd better not. Not if you know what's good for you. Let's follow her and see what she does."

Having seen the mortified janitor out, Maria went into the bedroom. She now put the box on the bed and took its contents out.

"Certificate of Distinction," she read out loud, "awarded to Clara Fini for Literature."

The name didn't ring a bell, and the date on the certificate was before Maria's birth. It was obviously a very old box, containing a girl's treasure, worthless to anybody but herself. She took an envelope and opened it. The paper was very brittle and cold to the touch. She removed the letter from the envelope and a black-and-white photograph fell out. Maria picked it up and looked at it. The girl on the left was obviously the same girl as in the other picture. The other was a plain girl of about the same age. She started reading the letter. It went,

> *"Dear Clara,*
>
> *It has been quite a while since you visited us. You may remember that on your visit Uncle took a*

*photograph of us. Here it is attached, hoping
that this will remind you of me.*

*What has become of the blue-eyed boy of whom
you spoke so much??? Are you still together?
Write back and throw us a bone, will you?*

*I will be leaving for school soon, and I'll miss
everybody here, but I hope to be back for the next
holidays.*

Be well and remember me,

Yours affectionately,

Rita"

"She has some nerve, reading my correspondence," Clara said. She had been reading it too, and George could tell that she was in the grip of strong emotions.

"Well, to be fair, I am sure that you would be curious too if you found a jewel box behind your boiler."

"That doesn't give her the right to read other people's private correspondence," she said, resentfully.

"Do I need to remind you that we actually *want* her to find out about you? We need her to know as much as possible about you, and to spread the word, in the hope that it will stir something."

"I know, I know. But I don't like it, all the same."

"It was your idea, so don't come to me with complaints."

"Well, there is one letter there that I don't care to have her reading. If she touches it, I will know what to do about it."

"Yes? And what is in that letter, if I may ask?"

"You may not, and it's none of your business. Now keep quiet and let's go on watching her." Clara was no longer joking now and, George could tell that she had undergone an extreme mood change.

"Who is that girl by the way?"

"She was my best friend, Rita."

"She looks nice."

"Yes. She died of cancer a few years ago."

"Oh, I am sorry."

"She had been ill for quite a while when I found out. And I spent a lot of time beside her–but, of course, she couldn't know I was there. You know, it was agony being there, and being unable to comfort her. But I decided that I would stay by her and see her through the last moments. Dying people can often see us and talk to us, and I was sure that I would be able to help her die peacefully, if only she would see me in her last hour. But, when the time came, she was so heavily sedated that she died in her sleep, and I never got a chance to talk to her. She must have been at peace with herself and gone through the meadow immediately, because I looked for her everywhere after she died, but never found her."

"Maybe you'll find her when you cross the meadow yourself."

"When? If–" Clara was silent for a moment and continued. "Somehow I have the terrible feeling that I have failed her. I was unable to do anything for her, to ease her pain, to soothe her fears. I waited there for months, and I was useless in the end."

"It wasn't your fault, you know."

"I know. But I was pretty useless all the same."

There was no good answer to that, so they went on watching Maria in silence.

Maria was looking at the letter. The signature was illegible, and the date was almost thirty-five years earlier. Nothing interesting here, Maria decided. She was starting to feel a little like an intruder, and all of a sudden she was ten years old again, searching through her sister's letters, fearful to be found out. Her sister had found her one day "snooping through her things," and her rage had been so terrible that Maria didn't care to remember it even today. As if brought back again to that day in her sister's room, Maria hurriedly folded the letter back into the envelope, returned the contents that were scattered on her bed to the box, and closed it. She would talk to Berto about it later, she decided.

Berto came home late as usual that night.

"Hi, honey," he called. "I feel so tired, that I'll better take a shower before I grab something to eat."

"Well, you can take as many showers as you want," she answered peevishly, "provided you don't mind doing it with freezing water, because that's all you get."

"Why, have you used up all the hot water? It doesn't matter, I can wait."

"Waiting will do you no good. There is no hot water, and what's more, there isn't going to be any. The boiler is dead."

"What do you mean 'dead'?"

"I mean gone, rotten, shut down. No water, not now, not tomorrow, not ever—until we replace that antique bomb that you call boiler."

"We have been through this before. We don't have the money to buy a new boiler."

"Well, suit yourself, but then we also don't have any hot water. And me, I am going to bed." She turned her back to him and marched into their bedroom without another word.

CHAPTER XVI
Exasperating David

"The scientific way to determine whether a death or a disappearance is due to natural causes is to collect sufficient data, which must be ordered in a logical sequence, and to analyze for patterns. Natural occurrences show a random behavior of many parameters, while a man-made death must present at least some ordered patterns. If we know how to look, we may find clues indicating that some occurrence is not rooted in natural causes."

David was giving his weekly lecture to a full auditorium. He stopped after this key sentence, trying to feel the pulse of the class, looking at them piercingly. Were they understanding the lecture? Why weren't they asking questions? The blank stares that his students returned to him did not give away their thoughts. Assuming they can think, he reflected bitterly. A lecture without questions always made him nervous. David was not adverse, on a good day, to admitting that he was so damn good that the reason why there were no questions was simply that he had been crystal clear throughout. Still, he was honest enough to acknowledge the possibility, however remote, that his students simply did not have a clue as to what the lecture was about.

His course on "The Logic of Murder" always attracted a large number of students. David liked to teach and to pass his passion for his pet subject on to others. What he disliked was preparing for the lectures. He prided himself on being able to lecture on everything at any time, without warning. Then, one day he had come to give a lecture, and too early through it he had realized that he had been left with nothing to say. His mind was a blank, and his lesson was supposed to last one more hour. In a panic, he had killed time by asking the students to express their opinions on axioms he had taught them before. His opinionated students, particularly the most stupid ones, found no difficulty in expressing their views at great length, on a subject they just heard of for the first time a few minutes before.

One student he particularly loathed–Botti was his name. It was not so much the fact that he would come to him at each break and after each lesson, and suck up to him, that alienated him to David. But it was the self-assured air of superior intellect with which he made the most appallingly wrong and idiotic statements that really jarred on him. There he was, time and again, asking diligent questions designed to impress on David his supposed intellectual depths. It was only a just retribution, David thought, that Botti should now work to get him out of this unpleasant corner of his.

"Botti," he had therefore said, "please give us your views on the impossibility to identify a clue that had been seen and not recognized twice before."

It had been agony for David to hear this obnoxious Botti embark in a meaningless tirade that mixed all his teachings, at the wrong places, with material that apparently belonged to some other course—a monologue that took the better part of fifteen minutes. Nevertheless this little trick had saved him from embarrassment, and he had been able to get back at Botti by summing up his discussion of the topic, thus, "A very good answer, Botti. I am sure that it will look even better when we find out what the question was."

He had reaped a good round of laughs from the class, and had saved face by stretching the lesson almost to its end—but he had promised himself that never again would he come to a lecture unprepared.

Last night he was so tired though, that he had almost gone to bed without preparing for today's class. It had taken him a great deal of willpower to go and sit by his computer instead, to prepare at least some transparencies to illustrate the various stages of his analysis. He had done so, falling asleep several times in between, and here he was, this morning, changing overheads with a self-satisfied feeling.

"As you will see, it is very important to keep to the right sequence of events when analyzing your data. I have summarized here," David said, changing yet another overhead, "the 'Ten Commandments' of this analysis. The first is, of course—"

David stopped, as a wave of laughter ran through the auditorium.

"I don't see what's so funny," he began, but stopped dead after reading the third line of his transparency. The lines ran as follows,

> 1–*Always order your data chronologically*
> 2–*Never mix data from different incidents*
> 3–*Don't forget Clara Fini*

There it was again! The same name, popping out of his computer. This is a conspiracy, he thought bitterly.

"Very funny, guys," he told the class, feigning an amused smile. "Someone has been playing around with my computer, as you see. Number three should have read–"

The lesson was finally over, not a moment too soon for David. He was now convinced that someone was playing dirty tricks on him. There was no other explanation. He had heard of computer viruses that were capable of doing virtually everything.

At the end of the lesson he hurried back to the main building. His own office was in another building, above the cafeteria, which was reserved for those lucky mortals who had their own cathedra, and who could afford a somewhat larger office than the complimentary standard cubicle issued by the faculty. All other faculty members nested in small offices in the main building. It was true that he had to pay the brigands of the Institute's treasury what practically amounted to a fortune for the extra elbowroom, but it was also true that, after all, it was Monsieur Lavoix who was footing the bill.

Mario, his colleague, was not "A Chosen One," and had a small office with the rest of the pariahs. You could hardly call it an office without blushing, as its dimensions were better suited to a closet. It housed a miniature desk that was almost entirely occupied by a computer screen and keyboard, and a small bookshelf overflowing with books and professional journals. In spite of the limited space, Mario did not seem to be able to throw away a single journal, so that the room was progressively closing in on him. David seldom visited Mario in his office because, as he used to complain, two people in there had to take turns breathing. Though normally well balanced and practical, he showed a predisposition towards claustrophobia and preferred to meet with his friend in the cafeteria. He got along well with Mario who did not seem to mind his pompous and somewhat irritating mannerisms, and he was the only faculty member upon whom he looked as a friend.

Today David was on the warpath. Someone had to pay for all the embarrassment and discomfort through which he had been put, and he was determined to find the culprit. He charged into the building and went straight to the corridor where Mario kept his office. Knocking on his door he was relieved at the "Come in!" that came from within. Mario was at his desk, apparently doing nothing in particular. He beamed a smile of welcome at David.

"Hi! What's up? Have you started calling on people also during the day? That's a nice change."

"I'm sorry about that," David said curtly, "but someone is playing tricks on me."

David had never been able to get over his belief that, no matter how grave the offence that he had inflicted on a person, all that was needed to repair it was a brief apology. It never crossed his mind that his apology might not be accepted, and he would have been surprised if someone had tried to get this notion across to him. So, after this sketchy apology, he went on.

"Do you remember what I told you over the phone, or were

you too sleepy to understand?"

Mario was too good-natured to take offense or bear a grudge for too long. It was due to this sunny disposition–and not, as David supposed, to his own magnetic personality–that Mario now answered amiably.

"I was wide awake, thanks to you. Thank you so much. And now what?"

"My computer keeps showing me the same name, no matter what I type. And it does it at random. And you tell me it's my imagination? My imagination, my foot. Today I found the very same name in the middle of a transparency that I prepared last night for today's lecture. Look here."

David held out the accused overhead for Mario to see, pointing at number 3.

"Are you positive that you are not typing this name unconsciously? These things happen, you know. I've often written a different word than I had planned to, because I was thinking of something else while writing. It is not uncommon with busy people."

"But I don't know this Clara Fini. Never heard of her. I don't know how she crept into my life, but I want her out of my computer. And now is not soon enough. You've got to help me, Mario."

"Have you checked your buffer? Maybe the name has somehow been saved in the buffer, and you paste it without noticing."

"I am not familiar with this 'buffoon' thing of which you speak," David said, waving away the notion with an irritated gesture, "and I doubt that I have any such thing in my computer. But I do know what 'copy–paste' is, and I use it all the time. I can assure you that there is nothing unusual there."

"Then this is serious, David. If it's not you, typing or pasting unconsciously, the next logical possibility is a virus. Probably a Trojan Horse. This behavior is due either to a very sophisticated virus, or to someone who has gained control of your computer through the data line. You are connected to the university network, aren't you?"

"Well, yes. But I never log-in, simply because I don't know how."

"It doesn't matter. It's sufficient that you're physically connected to the network, and anyone with access to it may get into your computer."

"So what do I do now?"

"First of all we need to disconnect your PC from the outside line. If someone is accessing it from the outside, he won't be able to go on intruding any longer. Then, we must run an updated virus check, and see if we come up with anything."

A troubling thought suddenly occurred to David, causing him to clutch at Mario's sleeve.

"Do you have any idea if this person, or virus, of which you speak can harm my files?"

"Certainly. It's very common that files are damaged or erased by viruses or intruders."

"Then we must rush to my house. All my work is on that damn computer."

"Don't you have backups?"

"No. Should I?"

Mario rolled his eyes to heaven. His friend was being too annoying for words.

"On which planet have you been before falling to earth? Of

course you should, you dummy."

"Well, teach me how. Later. Meanwhile, hurry. Get moving," David cried in panic.

Mario grabbed his coat and moved to the door, and there he was stopped by a new thought.

"Have you left the computer on?"

"Of course not. I always turn it off. I don't want it to burn the house down, or something, while I am away."

"Switch off the hysterics, then. We have time for coffee. Your intruder or virus can't work when the computer is off. Let's go to the coffee shop. I work much better with a couple of cups of black coffee in me."

"I'll make you coffee. Two cups, twenty cups. You name it. But let's rush," David said, pleadingly.

"Okay, okay, don't worry. We'll fix this in no time."

Mario left, leaving the room unlocked, and the lights on. This was his usual small revenge on the university cheapskates who believe that people can work in matchboxes.

David sat in the living room that doubled as a study, and watched Mario at work on his PC. He had been doing this for the last four hours now.

"How is it going?" David inquired.

"Good. Good. I think I'll find something soon," Mario said.

"Isn't that what you told me two hours ago?"

"Yes, yes. But now I think I see something. Let me run this virus check once more."

"I'm starving. Why don't we take a break and make some

sandwiches?"

"I like that 'we' state of mind of yours," said Mario. "As far as I can tell, you've been resting while I worked."

"There is no harder toil for the man of action than to watch somebody else working," said David. "I'd rather be doing what you do, if I only knew how."

"Yeah? Then go and make those sandwiches and bring them here. I don't want to stop now that I'm about to finish."

"Great! Are you going to be finished soon, then?"

"In a few minutes."

Mario's "few minutes" stretched until two in the morning, when he pronounced David's computer healthy and free from intruders and viruses.

"I'm baffled. There is no sign of a virus, and no file has been tampered with. It's a bloody mystery. This is something right up your street, not mine. Crime at the highest level," said Mario with a tired smile.

"So now what?"

"I don't know. Unless the people responsible for your computer's eccentric behavior are the CIA or the KGB, I would say that you are seeing things. I've tested every single bit in your PC, and nothing is the matter with it."

"Are you sure that you know what you're doing?"

"You are joking, right? Me? Knowing what I'm doing? I practically invented these PCs."

"I should've known that there was no point in looking for a rational explanation for the behavior of this diabolic machine. A pure waste of time, it was."

"Well, at least you know that there is no malicious program running on your PC. Whatever that was, it had nothing to do with it."

"A fat lot of good that does to me, if this blasted Clara F. keeps intruding into my work. We must find a way to stop it. What do you plan to do?"

"To begin with, I'm going to the bathroom."

David's house had very little in it to advertise his English origin. A small concession he had made to tradition was the bowl of potpourri that stood in the bathroom, on a small table near the door. It was a huge pewter bowl given to him by an aunt five years earlier, and its contents no longer emanated a pleasant scent. Still, David–although normally not a sentimental person, and perhaps quite the opposite–valued this bowl, which reminded him of his childhood house. This was why he kept the bowl in the bathroom, long after its contents had become no more than a mass of dry leaves and powder, and would not dream of throwing it away. He knew that sometime in the future the contents of that bowl had to go, but for the time being he was happy putting it off. It was this bowl that had almost caused David to dismiss his cleaning lady when, coming home one afternoon, he had found it empty. He had run to the dustbin in the kitchen and had discovered the contents of the bowl neatly heaped at its bottom. David had returned them to the bowl in the bathroom, and had waited for the arrival of the cleaning woman on the next morning.

"My dear lady," he had begun acidly, "could you please explain why you got it into your head to throw away my potpourri?"

"It was dry," the cleaning lady had said simply, "dry and dusty. And it smelled badly. That's why."

"I can't recall having asked you to be the judge of freshness of my potpourri, my dear lady," David had retorted. "I wish you would confine your activities to your well-defined duties, and refrain from taking uninvited initiatives. The potpourri is in perfectly good shape and has been reinstated to its bowl."

"Well, I know a smelly mess when I see one. That bowl stinks."

"I will trouble you," David had said icily, "to refrain from passing judgment on my belongings. I beg you not to touch that bowl again."

And this is where the argument had ended. Since then, David had made it his weekly practice to add to the bowl a flowery scent from a spray bottle he had acquired on the same day. He preferred to do so, however, when his cleaning lady was not around.

Mario knew nothing of the vicissitudes of the potpourri, and didn't notice it when entering the bathroom. But it was this very bowl that he proceeded to hit with his elbow, and it fell upside down on the floor with a deafening noise.

"What the hell was that?" inquired David who stood in the corridor by the bathroom.

"I'm sorry. I don't know how I could be so clumsy. I don't know what I was thinking, throwing my arm around like that."

The dry and brittle potpourri had been scattered by the flight of the bowl, and a large area of the floor was completely soiled. Mario went down on his knees, picking up the leaves with his hands. David knelt beside him to help, but soon they realized that this was not going to work.

"It'll take us ages in this way," David said. "I'll fetch a broom."

He got up, and Mario followed him. He took a step back

from the dirt, wiping sweat from his brow, and looked again at the mess he had made.

"David. Stop!"

It was a choking cry. David, already halfway through the door, turned back.

"Yes, what is it?"

Mario was looking at the floor, incapable of speech. His face was strangely contorted, as if he were struggling for breath. David followed his gaze. He saw the potpourri left on the floor, and the small part of it that they had managed to return to the bowl with their bare hands. And he saw something else. By moving with their fingers through the dirt they had created gaps in it, through which the off-white floor of the bathroom was clearly visible. The gaps in the dirt had the shape of block letters, and they clearly spelled six letters, *C-L-A-R-A-F*

CHAPTER XVII
Investigating

David was sitting at his desk when Mario came in. He had the annoying habit of entering without knocking, but David had given up any hope of correcting him. Not that he hadn't tried. Mario was carrying a daily newspaper in his hand and proceeded to wave it in David's face.

"I see that you have put an ad in the paper," he said.

The advertisement called for any person having knowledge of the whereabouts of one Clara Fini, who had disappeared on or around May 23, 1966, and for any person who had any information of any kind concerning her, to contact David. It gave his telephone numbers and included a faint promise of a reward, in the form of an unclear statement that any such person contacting him "would find that his time has been put to a good use."

On the night nicknamed by Mario "the potpourri night,"

they had sat until morning, talking about the strange phenomena that had invaded David's life, and hopelessly trying to make some sense out of them.

"I wish I knew who this Clara Fini is, anyhow," David had said.

"Why don't you put an ad in the papers?" Mario had suggested. "Maybe she'll answer it."

"You read too much fiction, Mario. People don't answer ads of this type. If you were a professional in this field, you would know that only point–oh–five–five per cent of all ads put in newspapers by the police ever get any real results. What you do get are crank calls, or people hoping for a reward, who send you on a wild goose chase. No," he had continued, shaking his head, "there are much more scientific ways of doing this."

"Yeah? I may not be an expert like you, but I still have some common sense, and I tell you that an ad might do the trick."

David had looked at him with forbearance. He found it trying that these dilettantes really didn't understand that investigation is a science.

Early next morning, after three hours of sleep and a frugal breakfast, he had left a message on a friend's machine at the investigative bureau of the city police, asking him briefly for his help in obtaining information concerning a certain Clara Fini. He was quite surprised when his friend called him back two hours later, to tell him that there was indeed a file bearing the name of one Clara Fini.

"There is a complaint filed by her mother, one Benedetta Fini, about her daughter's disappearance. It's an old complaint, filed in 1966. According to the record, she complained after her daughter hadn't come home, or called, for a week. Inquiries were made, which didn't lead to any results. The file is open, in temporary suspended status, pending resumption of the investigation if any new information warrants it."

David was amazed, for the hundredth time, at the police's notion of the meaning of the word "temporary." A file inactive for over thirty years, relating to a missing person, looked to him anything but "temporary." His guess was that this person was gone for good, whether voluntarily or involuntarily. But perhaps a "temporary suspension" was a good shield against the admission of defeat–something of which the police very much disapproved.

"I'll be there in one hour," he said. "Wait for me."

In fact, he got to the investigative bureau in forty minutes. It was a lucky break. He was confident that, now that some hard data had come up, the mystery would be unraveled in no time, and the person or persons who had been messing with his peace of mind would be found and prosecuted. He was in good mood now, feeling back in control again.

His friend was waiting for him with an inquiring look on his face.

"Hi. Do you mind telling me what this is all about?" he asked without any preamble. "Why are you taking an interest in this old case?"

"I can't tell you, right now. It's kind of personal, you know. But there is a slight chance that I may get some information on this case in the near future, and if I do I promise that you'll be the first to know."

"Has the old lady been feeding you nonsense?"

"What old lady?"

"The Fini mother. She'd been after us for years. This file is the nightmare of every section head who gets it. It has been going on for years now. As you can imagine," he lowered his voice confidentially, "we have given up hope of finding the subject, when she didn't show up after a few weeks. In these cases if you don't find a missing person within two months, it's a sure bet that you're never going to. She's probably dead, or perhaps she doesn't want us to find her. Either way, she's never going to turn up. Not thirty years after she has disappeared, and God knows what she looks like now."

"So why don't you admit it and close the file?"

"Can't. Standard procedure," he explained curtly. "We are not allowed to give up our search for a missing person, unless we have serious reasons to believe that he or she is dead. So we keep the case active, but stop searching. But can you explain this to her mother? Sure thing you can't. She keeps coming in and bugging us to look for her daughter, to find her body, to point at her grave. No can do! We don't have the time, the personnel, or the money to do it–plus, we don't have a clue on how to start. And why she thinks that we should waste taxpayers' money on this, rather than look for people who can still be alive, it's more than I can understand. I'm a little pissed about this, because the last time that she came here–about six months ago–it was my turn." He stopped and looked at David.

"What do you mean, by 'my turn'?"

"We take turns talking to her, you see, so that we can tell her the same things all over again. 'Our investigation is ongoing, ma'am', I told her. 'Certainly, we have not given up hope, ma'am'. Bullshit! We haven't done a thing on it for thirty years, except pushing the file around, and filling it with reports of her mother's visits. Well, I'll leave you to it. I am not supposed to, but I'll make an exception this time, because whatever you are doing, maybe you can rid us of this bloody nuisance. Don't remove anything from the file. If you need copies, call me. When you are done, leave the file on the desk. See you," he concluded, opening the door, "and keep me posted."

The Fini mother, David pondered. Now that's a thought. Maybe she is the one behind all this. Perhaps she has heard of me and she is trying to drag me into this investigation? But how? She must be a hundred, if a day, and she surely does not know how to play tricks with computers. Perhaps she has a relative–a nephew or something–who does. But why me, and how can she know about me? There were too many questions, David realized, and there wouldn't be any answers until he got to the bottom of it.

He opened the file, and a beautiful girl looked at him from the photograph that was pasted on the first page of the "missing person data sheet." It was a black-and-white portrait, taken by someone who clearly knew his job. Her face was three-quarters turned toward him, the light reflected from a short ponytail. Her lips were parted to give a hint of a smile, and her deep eyes gazed intelligently into his. The life-like illusion of the portrait was almost perfect, and for a whole minute he sat there looking at her, almost expecting her photograph to start talking. He then dug into the file.

The complaint was dated May 30, 1966, and the details had been inscribed, in an elaborate handwriting. Mrs. Benedetta Fini had reported her daughter as missing since one week before. Her daughter Clara, she had told the police, made a point of calling her by phone at least once a week. She had never skipped a phone call, but now it was two weeks since the last time she had called her mother. No, she did not have her address. Her daughter didn't want her mother to know where she lived. She had left home a few months earlier and had never come back, but she was a good girl–so Mrs. Fini explained–and didn't want her mother to worry, and that's why she always called on Saturday or on Sunday. Never on other days. Always on Saturday or Sunday. No, she had never consented to come back home or to meet with her mother, but had promised to do so as soon as her work will allow her. Her mother's pleadings had not helped. Still, she would never skip a phone call to her mother on purpose, and that's why Mrs. Fini knew that something terrible must have happened to her. Her last call had been on Saturday. Yes, the twenty-first of May, and she had waited patiently until yesterday, Sunday the twenty-ninth, before deciding that something was wrong. When her daughter had not called, she had come to the police station.

The file was full of reports on inquiries made by the police with the neighbors, a couple of friends named by the mother, and numerous other interviews with the mother herself. It was clear to David that this had been treated more as a run-away case than a forced disappearance, and that the police had not gone out of its way to investigate it. Since it had all happened so long ago, all trails were cold and probably entirely useless. He took down the last known address of the Fini mother, closed the file, and went out. There was little else for him to do at this point, and the mother was at least a starting point.

The address he was looking for was in the suburban area of the city that he did not know well. The taxi driver who took him there apparently was not familiar with it either, because he dropped him two buildings away from the right one. These were beehive buildings, over thirty stories high, each housing a staggering number of people. He walked swiftly and reached the one he was looking for. The apartment he needed was on a relatively low floor–the fourth floor–which was lucky since the elevator was out of order. It was almost noon now, and foul smells emanated from under the doors of the apartments he passed on his laborious climb up.

On the third floor he paused for breath. A door opened a little, showing an eye that looked at him through the crack. The door then closed again, and the noise of bolts being thrown told him that he had not passed the inspection. He hurried up, feeling uneasy and after what seemed to be more like a hundred floors he reached his destination. On the fourth floor David took a few seconds to regain control of his breath, and then knocked on the door. A movement from within told him that someone was at home, but apparently, whoever that was, had no intention of opening the door. He pushed the doorbell, although he had tried it before with no results, and this time it produced a short ring. The sound of feet dragging toward the door reached him, and with them fumbling noises at the lock. Eventually, the door opened to show an old woman. She was very small and walked bent almost at an angle, as old people do when they fall victims to arthritis.

"Mrs. Fini?" David asked.

"Shgone, to zhe ospiss," the old woman answered.

She spoke out of a toothless mouth, looking up at David but spitting at the floor.

"Gone, you say? Where?"

"To zhe ospiss, zhe ospiss!" She seemed irritated by this young man who could not understand such a simple explanation. "Shaint Maria Ospiss. With Anna, you know?"

David didn't know, and didn't care to. Mrs. Fini was apparently visiting with this Anna, and why this old wreckage assumed that he should know about her, was more than he could fathom.

"When is she due back?"

"Never."

"Never?"

"Never. I said." She started to close the door, but stopped, seeing his pleading gesture.

"Wait a minute, please. Do you mean to say that she no longer lives here?" Encouraged by a slight movement of her head that he interpreted as a nod, he continued. "Then she is living at the St. Maria Senior Citizen's Home, not just visiting there, isn't she?"

"Yesh, Yesh. Zhe Ospiss, like I told you. Well Goo'by."

With these words she seemed to view the conversation as concluded, and closed the door in his face. He heard dragging noises from within, indicating that she was painfully moving away from the door, and then silence. There wasn't much more that he could get from her, he reckoned, and he was longing for fresh air to flush away the smell of boiled cabbage that clung to his nostrils and, he was sure, to his clothes, right down to his underwear.

Out in the street again he realized that he was stranded in the suburbs, with no hope of finding a taxi. This was no taxi neighborhood, and the chance of one coming along was nil.

"Pardon me," he inquired of a young man who stood on the pavement near the entrance to the building, "where is the nearest subway station?"

"It's a thirty minutes walk," said the young man, "perhaps thirty-five. You have to walk down this street and turn right where the street ends near the public swimming pool, and then straight-ahead until you see the subway station. But you can wait here with me for the bus, if you want. Number one-oh-eight should be coming along in twenty-five minutes, if it doesn't skip this station. Sometimes they do," he added pensively.

"I'll walk, thank you," David said, and started in the direction of the subway line.

The trip to the St. Maria Senior Citizen's Home, a car ride of no more than twenty minutes, took David the best part of two hours. A nurse was sitting at the reception, looking bored.

"I am here to visit Mrs. Benedetta Fini," David said.

"Are you a relative?"

"A friend, really," David lied.

"This is not visiting time, you know. Visitors are not allowed until four o'clock. However, I can see that you came a long way, and I'm sure that you didn't know the rule. Did you know the rule?"

"No," David said humbly, "I am afraid that I didn't know the rule, or I would have come at the appropriate time."

This nurse, for some reason, reminded David of a traffic cop. His driving was somewhat reckless, and he had often found himself in the position of having to present his driving license to a reproachful cop and he had learnt through experience that the best way to talk to them was to look and act contrite. He instinctively acted the same with this nurse.

"'Cause we cannot have people breaking the rules here, or where would we be?"

"Of course," David assented, looking even more mortified.

"But since you're not breaking no rule–not on purpose, that is–I will take you to the old lady. She must be in her room. That's where she is most of the time. But I'm afraid I can't stay with you," she said, looking for a proper expression of disappointment on David's face, which he dutifully produced," 'cause I've got to go back to the reception. Wednesday, you know," she added, as if that explained everything.

"I am sorry to hear that," David said, "but I am grateful to you for taking me."

"Here you go. Let me know when you leave."

They had reached a door–one of a row with no names on them, only numbers. The nurse turned on her heels and left. From the door he could see the room. It had three beds, each with a little night table beside it. On the bed near the window– the only one occupied at the moment–sat an old woman. The top of her night table was crowded with statuettes of Jesus, Mary and the Child, and the apostles. A very large cross hung from her neck. She sat there in silence, looking out of the window. Her lips moved slightly, perhaps in prayer, or possibly she was a victim to Parkinson's disease. He came a little closer, certain that she had heard him coming by then, but she took no notice of him.

"Mrs. Fini," he called.

She raised her head and looked at him, showing no surprise.

"Do I know you?"

"No, we haven't met."

"What do you want?" she asked bluntly. She turned her

head away from him, and went back to look at the window.

"I am here to ask you about your daughter, Clara."

"I don't have a daughter of that name," she answered, without looking at him.

"I believe you did, Mrs. Fini."

"If your daughter ran away from you, without a word, and never came back, would you still count her as your daughter?"

"Maybe she didn't want to go. Maybe someone made her."

"Oh, yes. That's what she keeps telling me. But do I believe her, do you think? I certainly don't."

"So she has come back!" David was excited. This meant that he could talk to her and find out what this was all about.

"Yes. She does come quite often. In fact, she is there by the window right now, you see?"

Oh, God! She is mad, David thought. Hope left him as quickly as it had come. Still, this woman, mad or not, was his only link to her daughter, and it was imperative to try to get some information out of her.

"Mrs. Fini. Can you tell me where your daughter was before she left? Was she staying with you?"

"You see," she continued, as if not hearing him, "I was never a religious woman. But since I got here, I started praying. And do you know what I pray for? I pray to The Lord," she went on, without waiting for a reply from him, "that I may die in my sleep. I would like to go to bed tonight, and not wake up tomorrow. And I pray to Jesus Christ every day, every hour. Do you think that The Lord may do this for me? Do you think He may have mercy of me and grant me eternal sleep?"

"I am sure that The Lord, in His mercy–"

"Senior Citizen's Home, they call it. Don't let them fool

you! It's the anteroom of death. We seem alive, we act alive, but we are dying. This is a one-way street for us. There is no going back. So, if our punishment for our sins is that we are given a slow death, I figure that dying quickly, without pain, without fear, is a great present. So I pray The Lord to grant this small favor to me. You see?"

"Yes, yes. I wish you all the best, and I am sure that The Lord will hear your prayer. Now, Mrs. Fini, if you would please be so kind as to answer me. This is very important to me. I need to know. Could you please tell me anything about the whereabouts of your daughter before she disappeared? Who was she seeing? Did she have any close friends I could talk to? Anything that you could tell me would be helpful. Please?" he added pleadingly.

"But certainly, my dear," she said, smiling at him for the first time. "I don't remember much, but if this is so important to you, why don't you ask her?" she added, pointing at the window, "she must know."

David got up, with a sinking feeling, bade her a curt farewell, and walked out quickly. At the entrance, the nurse was busy talking over the telephone, and signaled to him to wait. He nodded without stopping, sliding by her through the door, and in a moment was gone.

"Yes, Mario," David admitted. "I did put an ad in the newspapers after all. I didn't want to disappoint you. Besides," he added truthfully, "I have no better idea. Lousy as yours is," he added sadly.

CHAPTER XVIII
A Lucky Break

Maria was in bed, reading her newspaper. She had seen the girls off to school, and her husband had left early for work.

The zealous little clerk, she thought bitterly.

She was resentful of his hard-working attitude. Never a complaint. Never concerned about himself. Always ready to sacrifice himself for his family. Always the perfect, loving, caring husband. Irritatingly so. Sometimes she thought that he was doing it on purpose, to annoy her and to spurn her laziness.

She knew that her own contribution to their life was small, but she expected him to do his best to make her feel all right with it. She was not ashamed of her way of life, purely because she was shameless. But his saint-like attitude irked her. It is true that he never said anything that even remotely sounded like a reproach, but she could tell that he *thought it*. He was patronizing her, she felt, by disapproving of her attitude, without saying a word. Sometimes she would flaunt her laziness by telling him how relaxing it had been to stay in bed until noon with a magazine. She wished he would say something that she could use to pick a fight–but no, he would just smile conciliatorily, saying that she deserved a rest, seeing how hard she worked at the pharmacy, and moving on to another subject. Fighting with Berto–never an easy task–had become almost impossible lately, as he was always ready to compromise and to take the blame for almost everything.

The janitor, who had been making himself useful that morning, came back from the kitchen, and sat on her bed, pushing a cup at her.

"Here, I've made you a fresh cup of coffee."

She paid no attention. Her eyes had been captured by an advertisement that read, *Do you know Clara Fini? Do you have any information concerning her or her whereabouts?*

The ad gave the name of a contact person, and added the appealing information that "any person calling with actual information would find that his time had been put to a good use."

Clara Fini. That was the name of the girl from the box, she was sure of it! She had forgotten all about the box until then, but it all came back to her. The photograph, the letters, and the name. And she was certain it was Clara Fini.

"Are you going to drink this coffee, or what?" asked the janitor.

"Yes, yes. Put it down. And put your shirt on, will you? I am a little busy right now. Come back later."

"Later? When?"

"I don't know. Like tomorrow, next week. Whenever. Just

be a good boy and run along now, okay?"

The janitor put on his shirt, obviously trying to look as hurt as possible. This was wasted on Maria, however, who was busy re-reading the ad for the fifth time.

She was amazed by the coincidence. She was sure that this must mean something. There must be money in it. People don't waste good money on ads merely for the fun of it.

Maria took out the red box from the drawer where she had dumped it, and promptly dismissed from her mind. Until now. She emptied it once again, carefully, almost religiously, looking at each item and searching for a hint to explain why this girl was so important to merit an expensive advertisement in a daily newspaper. Perhaps the box contained something of value that had been overlooked during her first cursory examination of its contents. The items did not teach her anything new, however. They were, exactly as before, trinkets, letters, and photographs. No map to a treasure, and no hint that a high-society scandal might be found somewhere in those letters. It was an exasperatingly ordinary box, such as many teenage girls keep. In fact, she herself had kept one very much like it in high school.

She picked up the phone and dialed the number listed in the ad.

"Yes?" said a voice at the other end.

"I am calling about Clara Fini," she said.

"Yes?" The voice was suddenly alert.

"I believe that I have some information that may be of interest to you."

Berto was waiting for the elevator. He was puzzled by Maria's call.

"Come home, Berto. This is urgent," she had said.

"What's the matter? What happened?" he had asked, a sudden fear rising in his throat. Maria had never before called him in the middle of the day–she knew how important and responsible his job was–and she had certainly never before asked him to leave in the middle of his work and come home.

"Nothing happened. Everything is okay, don't worry. But I need you to come as quickly as possible."

"Is this about the girls? Are they sick?"

"No. I told you everything is all right," Maria sounded exasperated, "but there is something I must show you and that we must talk about, and it can't wait."

"Look here, Maria. You know how difficult it is for me to leave during the day, and particularly now."

"It can't wait," she said curtly, and her tone left no room for argument.

So now here he was, at home in the middle of the day. He suddenly realized how little he had seen of his home in daylight. It felt odd, he thought. Almost as if he were a stranger in the building, an intruder. He took the elevator, impatient to learn his wife's reasons for summoning him so urgently. Maria was in the sitting room, talking to a stranger. They both turned to him when he came in.

"Berto, this is Dr–"

"Call me David, please," intervened the stranger. "I am a professor of applied history."

"Pleased to meet you," said Berto mechanically, looking inquiringly at Maria.

"My pleasure," said David, managing to look thrilled by

Berto's presence.

"Applied history, you said?" Berto was tempted to ask what applied history actually *was*, but thought better of it. "I wish you would explain what this is all about," he added, turning to Maria.

"I'll tell you," said Maria. "It all began with this old box here. Do you remember that we had a fi–...we discussed the boiler and whether we should replace it? It was on the same day that the janitor opened the cabinet behind the boiler to look for leaks in the gas pipe. When he did, he found this box that had apparently being left there many years ago. I didn't get around to mentioning it to you, because we were too busy–" she hesitated and then continued, throwing a glance at David, "–discussing whether to renovate the hot water system."

"Let me see it," said Berto, taking the box from Maria's hands. He opened it and examined its contents at length. "This is just an old box with photographs and letters," he said eventually. "There is nothing of value in here."

"I know. That is why I forgot to mention it to you. Actually, I forgot all about it, until this morning, when I saw this ad in the newspaper."

She handed the newspaper to Berto, who read the ad and turned to David.

"Did you put this in the newspaper?"

"Yes, sir. I did."

"Then I guess you will be able to explain this to us?"

"Well, yes and no."

"What do you mean, 'yes and no'? You do know why you posted it, don't you?"

"Oh, yes. Definitely. You see, I am a university professor, and I do research work on unsolved mysteries, such as murders, disappearances, etc. I have come across the name of Clara Fini during another project," he lied easily, "and from the information gathered in respect of that other project, it seemed that this person might have disappeared."

"What other project?" Berto asked suspiciously. He was not yet buying the story. His was a suspicious nature as far as strangers were concerned, almost as much as he was trusting with his own family.

"I am afraid that I am not at liberty to disclose the nature of this other business," David said, assuming his best official countenance, "since it relates to matters better kept exclusively among those authorized to know. In any case, my present investigation on the possible disappearance of Clara Fini is only incidental to that other business."

"I see," said Berto, who didn't, but refused to admit it.

"But wait until you hear the rest," Maria said, with a contagious excitement in her voice.

"We checked the police files, and found that one Clara Fini had been reported missing. According to our records, she was never found." David was beginning to enjoy the sense of official importance that his story was creating around him. He had been quite clever; he complimented himself, by hinting at his imaginary official role, without actually compromising himself.

"We now know that, at some time in the past, she had access to these premises. We hope, with your permission, to be able to search your apartment and find additional clues that may help us solve this–uh–intriguing mystery. We would be ready to pay you for your permission and, of course, for any damage that we may cause."

"Damage?" asked Berto, alarmed. "Why should you cause

damage?"

"Well, you see, sir," (the use of 'sir' was always helpful to ease the tension), "this box was hidden behind the boiler. If she, or anybody else, hid anything else, it would not be in sight, otherwise you would have found it a long time ago. We must therefore look for clues in unusual places. For instance, we may have to remove a few ceramic tiles."

"You want to take my bathroom apart?"

"I can assure you that we will cause the least possible damage, and only in cases where it is absolutely necessary. And for whatever damage we may do, we will pay handsomely. My research fund has the money to finance this work, and I am ready to spend it."

"You see, Berto," Maria was clasping her hands as if she were a little girl, "if they have to take the bathroom apart, it's the best thing that could happen to us. We will finally have the money to pay for a modern bathroom, with piping that doesn't make noises and doesn't leak. Not like the one we have now."

"And I will pay for the time and any arrangements. Your wife and children may want to move out for a few days, and of course, the hotel bill will be taken care of by us. Nevertheless, I would like you to stay to supervise the work personally, and to make sure that nothing is done against your will. What do you say?"

"Well, I don't know." The idea of having strangers around the house, invading their privacy, was not appealing to him. Although he knew that they could use the money. "I would like to have a word with my wife in private, if you don't mind."

"Of course. Please take your time."

"What do you think you are doing?" he asked in an angry

whisper, having dragged Maria into a corner of the room. "I don't want any strangers looking into our things and having the run of the house."

"They are not interested in our things. They are looking for something that may have been hidden in this house thirty years ago. They are not going to look through our stuff."

"But he wants to take the place apart. He wants to break tiles, and probably to demolish walls. Why should we let him do it?"

"For the money, stupid!" Maria said, barely able to keep herself from shouting at him. The idea that they should refuse the money that was being offered by this crazy professor was appalling to her.

"And for a little money I should stay home to watch over these people, and perhaps miss my chances of a promotion? I'm not doing it! I'll tell him to go.

"Professor—" he started, moving in David's direction.

"We will pay this sum in advance," David said, handing Berto a check. The sum was enough to rebuild the whole apartment twice over.

"We'll do it," Berto said.

"Oh, honey!" Maria said. An expression she seldom used for Berto.

Berto was walking around the apartment. Their furniture had been dragged to the center of each room, and was covered with white sheets for protection. The sheets gave the whole house a ghostly feeling that made him uneasy. The contents of the cupboards had been emptied, in an orderly fashion, into boxes, and all the pictures had been removed from the walls then neatly stacked under the sheets. The house looked cold and unfamiliar. Two small men in gray coveralls were running about with tools— looking too damn efficient, he thought. He had regretted already several times the foolish impulse that had caused him to agree to this nightmarish process. Maria seemed so keen, though, that he hadn't had the heart to disappoint her. And the money was good. Still, he wished they would find whatever they were looking for, and go away.

At first, he had attempted to keep control over things. He had tried to reason with one of the two men, (whom he had come to think of as "the demolition men"), and to convince him that there was no need to remove the chandelier.

"What are you doing that for?" he had asked, pointing at the chandelier.

" 'S my job," was the answer.

"It is *not* your job to ruin my property for no purpose," Berto had argued.

"Hey," the man had answered cheerfully, " 's not my place to decide. I'm the hired hand. You should talk to the professor."

Berto had talked to the professor.

"What is your man doing?" he had asked. "What is that in aid of?"

"We are looking for clues, as I explained at least three times already."

"You said that you were looking for something that a girl might have hidden. No girl could have hidden something above the chandelier," he had appealed to David.

"We can take nothing for granted, Berto," David had said.

He had taken to calling him "Berto" rather than "sir," once

their little contract had been signed. That little contract that he had not read, Berto had belatedly discovered, contained a fat damages clause setting forth heavy penalties for Berto, if he should back out of their agreement. Outraged by the dismantling of a windowsill, Berto had decided at the very beginning of David's investigation to return the check and kick everybody out.

"Leave immediately," he had shouted in rage. "And take those two Cossacks that you have brought into my house with you. I will have your check returned first thing in the morning."

"Read paragraph fourteen," David had suggested.

"Ah?"

"Paragraph fourteen of the contract. Read it."

Berto had read paragraph fourteen. Paragraph fourteen listed at least seven penalties that Berto might incur as a result of any act that might be considered a breach of contract. It seemed that virtually everything, except keeping quiet, was a breach of contract, according to the paper that he had signed. And he did not care to run up against any of the penalties listed in paragraph fourteen. That very same clause was now preventing Berto from kicking David and his two demolition men out, in spite of their continued and aggravated provocation.

A sound of breaking tiles came from the bathroom, causing Berto to start.

"What the hell are they doing there?" he demanded of David.

"We are removing a few tiles, Berto, just as I told you we might have to do. Yes," David shouted back, replying to a query coming from the bathroom, "you can remove the sink."

"What? What!!" Berto cried in anguish. "Are you mad?

You are taking my home apart!"

"And paying you very well for it, I should say."

There was little that Berto could do or say. It had been folly to accept this man's conditions, but now it was too late to do anything about it. For the first time in his life, something resembling resentment for Maria's selfishness started to creep into his mind. He fought to keep it back, but with little success.

The noise of breaking tiles continued, causing Berto's already low spirits to sink even lower.

"Cheer up," David said. "We are doing you a favor, really. I don't know how you managed to live in this shabby apartment for–how long was it?–doesn't matter. Years, anyway." Berto did not answer. He had decided to ignore this person, whom he found extremely objectionable. Also, in deference to paragraph fourteen, he bravely fought the impulse to punch him on the nose–an impulse that he had had several times since he first met David. Paragraph fourteen did not permit "violence inflicted upon the academic personnel and/or its supporting staff."

David, in contrast, was in good mood. He felt it in his bones that they were about to get somewhere. That box was a clear sign that more was to be found. Until anything was found, however, there was little for him to do, and tormenting Berto seemed to be as good a pastime as any.

"Now you will be able to buy your little wife the new little kitchen she has been dreaming about," David said with a smirk. "Isn't that great?"

Berto did not answer. He glanced at David dangerously, almost forgetting paragraph fourteen, but did not move.

"Professor!" an excited voice came from the direction of the bathroom, "Come here, quick!"

David ran to the bathroom in excitement.

Berto ran in pursuit. He could do nothing to stop these acts of vandalism, but he was decided to make sure that they did not cause unnecessary damage. He ran into the bathroom and stopped, flabbergasted. It looked like a construction site. The sink had been removed and thrown into a corner. A large number of tiles had been ripped off and broken. And the bathtub itself had been lifted and moved aside. Sand and debris from under the bathtub were scattered around, adding much to the feeling of destruction. And from the basis of the tub something was sticking out.

An undefined object.

Berto approached the remains of his tub to take a closer look.

He looked.

Then he fainted.

CHAPTER XIX
Shopping?

Maria was window-shopping–or like a friend of hers had once put it, she was guilty of "window-shopping with intent to buy." This was quite different from her regular window-shopping that was devoted to goods bearing such price tags that she knew she would never be able to afford, which included Jaguar cars, designers' items and diamonds. This time she meant business. She hadn't had that much money in her hands for years, and the feeling was inebriating.

She had cashed David's check at the bank, and the money was now nesting happily in her bank account. Her own account, for sure. After their marriage she had insisted in keeping her own separate bank account, to which Berto had no access and over which he had no power to nag her, and she was now glad of it.

"But, honey," Berto had argued, "we are one, remember? All we own belongs to both of us, so why keep a separate account?"

"Oh, I don't know. Just so that I feel better. Do you mind?"

"But it doesn't make *me* feel better. It feels as if our marriage is incomplete. As if we keep secrets from one another."

"Don't be silly. It's simply that I need some time to get used to having lost my individuality. Only a little while longer, okay?"

"I don't really mind," Berto had lied. "But you know, the bank fees that come with it," he had feebly tried to argue, "they are very high, and I really feel that we don't need any more expenses right now."

"Just a little longer, okay?"

"Yes, but–"

"Just a little longer."

There the matter had rested. Berto had acted offended for a while, but she didn't care; she needed her freedom to spend money–and perhaps to save some–without her husband's petulant interference.

Berto liked projections, calculations, balance sheets, interests, and all that rubbish. He would spend evening after evening drawing curves on paper with his pencil, and proudly presenting the results to an uninterested Maria. She knew that none of her husband's forecasts had ever come even close to reality, and in all likelihood never would. Still, he would insist in wasting his time in producing these useless pieces of paper. That was where his masculinity resided. There he was the real dominator and the master of the house, she often thought bitterly.

Maria hated any single piece of paper that came from the bank, and religiously refused to read bank correspondence, which regularly found its way to the wastepaper basket in small pieces, together with the unopened envelope that contained it. Her relations with the bank were limited to the depositing of money, and its withdrawal. Occasionally she would consent to talk to a clerk, if he telephoned her to call an overdrawn account to her attention, or to hint at any other misbehavior on her part–but she always did so hastily and ungraciously.

But today she loved her bank. Well, not the bank itself, perhaps, but what was in it–and in her own personal account, she reminded herself. It was true that the money was intended for the renovation of the apartment, and that she was not supposed to spend any substantial part of it on anything else; but there was so much of it.

Oh, God! she thought, quickening her pace and almost hopping joyously, There is so much of this fool's money! Thank you, God. Thank you!

This professor character was obviously a fool. He had been boring her stiff for two hours with idiotic stories about what he insisted on calling "applied history", as if it meant anything, until Berto had finally got home and rescued her from boredom. Her instinct had told her right away that it would be wise to ingratiate herself with this pompous ass, and she had acted the wide-eyed innocent girl, taken in by his tales of suspense. "Oh, my dear! That is so very clever!" she had exclaimed when he had told her about the way he collected data on long-gone murderers; and she had let out an excited "I don't believe it!" when he had explained to her about something he called a "clue matrix". He seemed happy to explain all this to her accompanied by sporadic sounds of appreciation from her, that required little or no attention on her part. She had been making calculations, all the while trying to figure out how much money she should ask for giving him the run of the house.

She had insisted on cashing the check before giving David permission to touch her apartment. She was no fool, and where money was concerned she didn't trust anybody, professor or not. David had not resisted, though, and had handed the check over to her without any argument. The check was good, and the cashier had paid it without a murmur.

Maria looked through the window of a fur boutique. She had never owned a fur, and that mink looked so gorgeous on that mannequin. She stepped in.

Silvia and Sandra were playing hide-and-seek in the park with friends. At first, Sandra had been a little surprised when, invited by one of the boys, Silvia had readily accepted. She was waiting for the usual "maybe later" answer, and instead her sister had joined them and was now playing as she had never seen her play.

"What's the matter, Silvia?" she had asked when they both paused behind a tree to catch their breath. "Aren't you going to the tower to work on your story?"

"No. I'm finished with the last one, and I don't feel like starting a new one. Not right now, anyway. Let's go catch them," she added, pointing at two of the boys who were running behind nearby trees, and starting to run in their direction.

Soon they were immersed in their game. Sandra had always kept an eye on her sister, almost like a mother watching her child play, to make sure that she would not forget herself at the tower, or go near that dangerous lake. She shot a glance at the tower now, out of habit, almost expecting to see her sister there. But she was by her side. Silvia had abandoned her daydreaming. The fables no longer appealed to her. And she definitely was not going to go to that tower yard again. Ever.

David was talking to the policeman. He was trying to explain the fine scientific reasoning that had brought him to this apartment, looking for clues and ending in the discovery of a mummified body turning up in the most improbable of places. He was not telling him all the truth about the reasons for his investigation. He had just realized that telling the whole truth about the strange chain of events that had brought him here could make him look odd. He particularly objected to looking odd. Looking odd did not befit his professorial dignity.

"Look here, Officer," David said, impatiently, "I did put all the clues in an appropriate matrix, and concluded that there might be something of interest in this apartment."

"Yes. I heard you saying that," said the policemen, "but *how* did you come to be here?"

David raised his eyes to the ceiling. Talking to this flatfoot was proving a trying experience. Moreover, he was polishing his story while telling it, taking into account how it would look to the academic world, and how better to put himself in the proper light.

He was considering the opportunities that presented themselves in this situation. It was not often that his theories produced results on such an impressive scale, and he was not going to let this opportunity slip between his fingers.

"I told you," he said for the fourth time, "I put all the clues together and reached a conclusion. Something, I may add, that you people were supposed to be doing," he added pointedly.

"Did you know the victim?"

"Officer. *Officer*," David said compassionately. "Have you *looked* at it?" The body itself was still hidden within the sand, but the protruding hand was telling the tale. "I ask you, have you looked at it? Even a child would understand, judging by the state of the hand and of the fabric, that she has been there for decades. How would I know her? I was probably not even born when she found herself used as a tub stand."

"I am told that you paid a very large sum to the owners of this apartment," the policeman said, pointing with his pencil at Berto who was sitting on a nearby chair, shaking. He had been shaking for quite a while now, since he had regained consciousness. He now rose and walked toward them.

"Do you know how many times I have taken a bath in there?" he said, his voice shaking with rage and fear. "And all the while she was in there, wasn't she? I have washed my babies in there, with her buried there."

His voice broke, and he looked at David with hate.

"It was you. I know. I don't know why and how you did it, but it's all your doing, you bastard."

"Please, sir," the policeman said. "I understand your feelings. I appreciate that you are overwrought right now, but I must ask you not to interfere with our investigation."

"I don't want to interfere. I just want to kill him for what he has done to us."

The policeman moved aside to shield David from Berto, intercepting with his hand, without effort, a punch that Berto had feebly directed at David.

"I didn't do anything, my dear man," began David, "I

merely–"

"Shut up!" said the policeman.

"Ah?"

"I said, shut up."

"But–"

"Shut your trap, Professor." He somehow managed to make the "professor" sound like something dirty. "And you, sir," he continued in a conciliatory tone, turning to Berto, "go to your room and lie down. We don't need you to go to pieces now. I will be talking to you again later."

Berto, now docile again, turned away, and the policeman resumed his questioning.

"Now, is it true that you paid such a large sum for the right to do with the apartment whatever you please?"

"Not whatever I please. I paid to conduct research, of course within academic boundaries."

"Why did you pick this apartment, and how did you know that the body was here?"

"I put an ad in the newspaper, and these people called me. I didn't know that the body was here."

"What is the nature of your acquaintance with the victim?"

"I don't know her at all."

"If you didn't know the victim," the policemen asked, not unreasonably, "how did you know that you should be looking for her body?"

David was not stupid. He realized that there was no way to explain away his interest in the case. The truth had to be told.

"I'll tell you, Officer. It all started with a name suddenly appearing in my computer."

David explained at length all the occurrences that had led

him to initiate his investigation. He was surprised and pained to see that his explanations met with an unsympathetic, frosty eye.

"I fear that you shall have to explain this again to the Inspector at the station. We shall go there in a few minutes, when I'm through with my initial inspection."

"I may tell you right away that I have no time to waste, Officer," David started, with a ring of indignation in his voice. "I don't need incompetent police clerks to waste my precious time, when I could be out there, solving the mysteries that *you* should be working on. I hardly think it's your place to interfere with an academic of my–"

"Sergeant!" bellowed the policeman. David was taken aback and stopped in mid-sentence. A heavy-bodied policeman, whose presence David had previously failed to notice, stepped toward them.

"We are taking this alleged professor to the station for further questioning, as soon as I'm finished with the corpse," he said. "Stay with him, and if he breathes out of line, handcuff him." He turned on his heels, leaving an astounded David behind.

Silvia was standing by a tree, resting a sore foot. She had run too much for her–something that did not appear to bother her sister. Her gaze rested on the entrance to the Tower. It still held an attraction for her, but she was determined not to go there. A movement caught her attention. The woman was standing under the arch, looking at Silvia. She raised a hand, as if waving to her, then she turned around and was gone.

Silvia shrugged the appearance away, deciding that she had

been imagining things. Nobody was there, and there had never been, she convinced herself. She looked fondly at her sister who was running after one of the boys. She smiled unconsciously. She had a feeling that she was catching up with Sandra and may become practical yet.

The woman was sitting on the asphalt of the highway. She was crying in pain and in shock. The wreck of her car stood with its wheels in the air. Beside it, a fire brigade car was washing the road. The jet of water, she noted, was sweeping away a myriad of items that had been scattered from her car when it had flipped over several times. She watched her belongings being washed away, in a detached, impersonal way, as if she had nothing to do with them. A paramedic was bandaging her head.

It should hurt more, she thought. She was almost annoyed. Why doesn't it hurt more? It should hurt much more.

An ambulance was standing nearby, and the medics were lifting a bundle on a stretcher into it. That bundle, she realized calmly, was her husband. Yes, it definitely was her husband. So why are they lifting him into the ambulance? she wondered. And the medics, she noted, were in no hurry.

Her head had started to hurt badly now.

Thank God it hurts, as it should, she thought, rather incoherently.

She closed her eyes trying to drive away the pain.

The young man stood at the edge of the shopping center. He could not remember how he had gotten there. The last picture he remembered was that of himself on the highway, driving home together with his wife.

He was not familiar with this place. A long double row of shops ended in an open restaurant, with tables scattered around in a semicircle. He was standing beside one of the last tables, which was neatly covered with a red-and-white checkered tablecloth.

The young man was confused. He had heard of people experiencing loss of memory, but having this happening to himself was something else. He tried to remember what he was doing there, but no matter how hard he tried, no recollection came. One moment he was driving home, and the next he was standing there. The interval between was a total blank.

An old man was approaching him, and he scrutinized his face closely. He seemed to be vaguely familiar, but he was unable to place him.

"Ah, it's you, my boy. I was hoping to see you one of these days," the old man said. He took the young man by the elbow and motioned him toward one of the farthest tables. "Let's go and sit down together. No need, uh–to be formal now. You are a grown man now. Sit, sit. I will sit with you."

A faint recollection was now dawning on the young man. This must be his old school teacher. He hadn't seen him in ages.

The young man was annoyed. Why did the old bore think that he was entitled to stop him like this in the street, and what's more, on a day like this? The teacher was talking and talking, and the young man was trying to focus on what he was saying. He was doing so with some difficulty, but eventually the words started getting through to him.

"Do you remember what I used to tell you in first grade?

That you all were my children…"

Maria walked along the street. She had not bought the mink, after all, and was feeling miserable because of it. She knew it was all Berto's fault. He was such a miser, that she couldn't buy herself anything.

Suddenly, a movement caught her eyes. A small girl was walking before her, and was now turning into a narrow alley. The girl looked familiar. She knew that sweater and skirt; she had laid them out herself that very morning. And she could not mistake her hair, even from behind.

"Silvia!" she called.

The girl quickened her pace and disappeared into the alley. Maria ran after her and turned into the dark alley. The sound of Maria's steps echoed between the high walls between which the alley ran in what seemed to be a semicircle. The walls were mostly windowless, and the few windows they had, were firmly closed. The sound was amplified to an almost unbearable volume.

Maria felt uncomfortable, claustrophobic in the narrow space. The pungent stink of urine rose in her nostrils, making her feel sick. She could not understand what Silvia was doing, running away from her like this, unless she hadn't heard her. But what was she doing in that alley, so far away from home and all alone? She slowed down, short of breath. The alley was dead-ended, blocked by a high brick wall. Silvia was standing, her back to her, looking at the wall. Maria came close, still puzzled by her daughter's behavior.

"Silvia!" she called again.

Silvia turned slowly toward her, silently, not saying a word. Now Maria could see her face. It was not Silvia.

"Hello, Maria," she said in a low, rasping voice. A voice that had been rendered raucous by smoke and cancer. "Enjoying your shopping?"

David was unhappy. Miserable was perhaps a more accurate description of his mood. He had been brought handcuffed to the police station, after a determined but hopeless attempt to assert himself, by leaving the room without permission. His photograph had been taken, not only by the police, but also by a horde of newspapermen who were waiting for news on the new crime, a particularly hideous one, so they were given to understand, on which the police had stumbled. And David, so it was whispered, was the chief suspect.

David's humiliation was compounded by the physical discomfort, and by the fact that he had been totally ignored by everybody since getting there. His repeated demands to call his friend from the Missing Persons Department had only elicited silence and cold stares.

He would have considered all this small discomfort, though, had he only known what was in store for him. He was yet to see the headlines that the newspapers were printing, featuring his photograph as a handcuffed murder suspect.

"I don't know why the police do nothing about these drunkards," said the woman. She was wearing an obviously expensive fur and walked elegantly on high heels. Her companion was equally well dressed in a gray business suit and impeccable tie. "Look at this woman! She must be no more than thirty, and she has already drunk herself into such a state."

The woman was sitting on the sidewalk, leaning against the wall. Her hair was white and partly stood on end. At first sight she looked over sixty, but a closer look revealed a much younger woman. It was her expression and bearing that gave the illusion of old age. She stared before her with fixed, empty eyes, mumbling unintelligible words.

"What is she saying?" asked the woman.

"I don't know. I think she's calling a name, 'Silvia', but I can't understand what else she is saying."

"Let's walk quickly," whispered the woman, shivering and tightening her grip on the man's arm. She would have found it unpleasant to have that person beg her for money. She averted her gaze. Her mother had taught her that unpleasant sights should not be stared at.

CHAPTER XX
Letting Go

She found him standing by the window of the café, looking out toward the same old building. The late afternoon light was casting long shadows on the street, and the two policemen that stood guard before the building shivered. In spite of the nice spring days he knew that the evenings were still cold. The entrance to the building was guarded, and documents had to pass hands before anybody was admitted within. He was watching all this activity in amazement. Everything about his old home interested him, and this burst of activity, in a small and otherwise usually sleepy street, was something new to him.

"George!"

He turned at the sound of her voice.

"Here you are!" Clara said. "I was hoping to find you here."

"What's going on over there?" he asked. "What is all this police activity about?"

She was actually smiling. A broad happy smile. She raised her hand, her fingers extended in a "V" sign.

"We have made it! It has worked. I heard them talk. They found a body in an apartment they were refurbishing–your apartment. They sealed the door, and tomorrow they will finish all their tests and analyses, and remove it. They are releasing no details, but I bet they found the body under the tub, as in your dream."

He felt a chill along his spine. Could it be that his dream was true, after all?

"So what do we do now? It's out of our hands." For the first time since they had started trying to uncover the truth, he sounded entirely lost.

"Don't you see? If it's me, I will know. And you will know. And we can let them bury me and your nightmare, and we can go away. However, we must do it now. We must go up to your apartment now, and see."

A sudden fear got hold of him. A familiar fear. Many years before he had been invited by a friend to go gliding. His friend had bought this new glider that seated two. You would sit in it, hooked to an airplane with a cable, and it would drag you up into the air and leave you there all alone, without an engine and in total quiet, to glide yourself back to safety. On TV it looked easy, and he had gratefully agreed to take a ride. During the whole week he had been excited, in anticipation of the bird-like feeling. He had prepared himself thoroughly, trying out clothing and gear, and on the morning of the next Sunday, at the appointed time, he had stood by the glider in the grip of an insurmountable terror.

"Get in," his friend had said.

"Can we wait a few minutes?" he had asked.

"What for?"

"I–I need to go to the bathroom before we leave."

"No time for that. Save it for when we get back."

"I can't. Just five minutes." He knew he had to put it off. Even for five minutes; for a minute. But not now. Not right now, please. Just a little longer.

He had eventually got into the glider, and had enjoyed himself immensely, but for some reason had never wanted to go back and do it again, in spite of renewed invitations from his friend.

This was how he felt now. He knew that he had to do it. He had to face the truth about his dream, his father, his life, and the feelings that had accompanied him for all those years. But not yet. Not right this moment.

"I know how you feel," she said, as if reading his thoughts. "I'm scared too."

She took his hand and looked into his eyes.

"But you know that we must do it, don't you?"

"Yeah. I know. Only I wish we didn't have to."

"This is our only chance. If they take the body away, we may never get another opportunity to see it as they found it. And the newspapers may not print all the details. Sometimes the police keep vital details secret, so that they may verify the reliability of new information as it becomes available. So it may be now or never."

He looked at her, thoughtfully.

"And there is something else."

"What?" she inquired, eyeing him inquisitively. "What?"

"Assuming that we are right, and that it is you up there,

buried under the tub. What happens next?"

"I guess that there will be nothing more for us to do here, and that we will be able to cross the meadow, at last."

"Exactly. And what will happen then? To us, I mean."

"I don't know. How would I?"

"But you know that it is possible that we shall never see each other again."

"Yes, I know that." She looked at him pensively. "But I hope that we will. I don't know exactly what happens when you cross the meadow, but I have heard that people do get reunited."

"But if we don't, I'll miss you. Sorely. I have gotten used to having you around, and I can't imagine going on without you, right now."

"I, too, have given much thought to you–to us–since we met," she said fondly. "And the funny thing is to think that something good has come out of our misfortunes."

"How do you figure that?"

"Think of it. If it weren't for my untimely death, you would have always remained a child to me, and perhaps under other circumstances, even my stepson. I would never have come to know you as I do now, as a warm, caring man. And I would have missed the opportunity to know how it feels to be so close to you. Do you realize that?"

"The thought had crossed my mind. I don't think that I would have liked you as a stepmother, though. I prefer you as you are now."

"So do I." She mused for a while, and then continued, "Let's take a vow to look for each other after we cross the meadow, and to look after each other when we are there. How would you like that?"

"How would I like that?" For the first time George was finding it difficult to speak. "Look, I don't know what happens–or where one gets to–after crossing that meadow. I have no idea of what I will have to do then, but sure enough I want to do it with you. You want a vow? Here is a vow, If I can find you on the other side, I'll stick to you until you are sick and tired of seeing me."

"It's a deal," she said with a smile, "and I wouldn't have it otherwise. Now what about getting going?"

"Not so soon. There is time yet. They have sealed the house and they won't be moving anything till morning. Why don't we sit here for a while longer and enjoy our last date at this café?"

"All right by me. Put your arm around my shoulders, will you? That's better," she said when he did it. "A girl needs some attention, every now and then."

"Do you like poetry?"

"I used to," said Clara, surprised. "Why do you ask?"

"I was thinking of an acquaintance of mine. I wonder if they have books of poetry where we are going. If they do, I would like to read some to you."

"Is that another vow?"

"You may call it that. And also a tribute to someone I knew."

"I wouldn't make too many promises if I were you, George, 'cause I plan to call on you to fulfill every one of them. Now I really think that we should be going," she added, rising quickly before he could think of any new way of putting it off.

He did not have the time to object that the apartment was sealed, and that he did not know how to enter, which was the only feeble excuse that came to his mind. "We do not affect matter," she had said once, and she was right. She took him by the hand, and in a moment they were standing in the hall of the apartment in which they had spent so many hours together during the last weeks. It was now stripped of its furniture, but still looked painfully familiar to him. They stood hesitatingly in the corridor, before the door leading to the bathroom.

"Let's go in, George," she said.

"Are you sure that you want to go through with this?"

"Yes. Just don't let go of my hand, please."

They entered the bathroom. Here, in the corner, someone had thrown aside the tub in which he'd had endless baths as a child. Its base still stood untouched—a frame of bricks and rubble, filled with sand. And from that sand a mummified human hand protruded. The rest of the body was mercifully hidden by the sand that the police had returned to its original position after a first superficial inspection of the body, but there was no doubt that it was there.

"Look at the bracelet!" she cried. "It's mine! Here, look for yourself." The bracelet on her hand was the same as the one on the body. It was a unique jewel—a golden chain with enamel figurines of elephants and bears. A childish jewel, but a distinctive one. "It was your father's gift to me," she said, "when I agreed to come and live with him. 'A baby's bracelet for my baby lover', he joked when he gave it to me. I loved it. I wonder why he didn't remove it before he buried me."

Suddenly a memory of that jewel flashed before his eyes. She was right, he had seen it before. It was on the wrist of the woman of his nightmare. His dream ran before his eyes as a movie, the frames slowing down to show the bracelet disappearing below the sand that his father was pouring over the body. It was then that his father had turned and seen him. His father's sweaty face had turned toward him, and he had spoken to him curtly.

"What are you doing here? Why aren't you in bed?"

"I–I have to use the bathroom. It woke me up. Can I, now, please?"

"How long have you been standing here?"

"I just got here. I can't wait any longer. Please."

"Go ahead, but be careful not to trip over this equipment here."

He had run to the toilet bowl to relieve himself under his father's watchful eyes.

"Why are you working so late, Papa?" he had asked. His father was an aristocratic figure, and he was not used to seeing him dealing with menial tasks.

"I had to fix the bathtub. A leak. We can't be without it even for one day. The plumber couldn't come today, so I had to fix it myself." He looked at George thoughtfully, and added, "You are not to tell anybody that I did the work myself. I don't want to offend the plumber. Do you understand?"

"Yes, Papa," he had said, half asleep already, and had gone back to his room. The significance of what he had witnessed had not hit him immediately, but he had apparently being thinking about it subconsciously, and that was why his nightmare had started a few weeks later. Yes, now he remembered it all, clearly and vividly.

"Can we get out of here, please?" he said, pleadingly. He no longer wished to stay and contemplate the last ruins of his father's image. The relief of having gotten to the roots of his nightmare was heavily balanced by the sadness of their discovery.

"Yes. There is nothing more for me to do here now. I am now at peace with myself, and I can let go of this world. I think that I will take a walk across the meadow now. Are you coming too?"

"No," he said, suddenly animated by a new thought, "I have another little bit of business to take care of, before I do. There is at least one wrong that I can put right before I go. Then I'll feel good about crossing the meadow."

"I will be going now, then," she said. She blew a kiss at him and, for the first time, he saw her smiling a real, wholehearted smile. "Be well, and don't stay behind for too long. I'll be waiting for you."

With these last words she turned and walked down the corridor, and was soon gone.

The bartender was still at the bar, cleaning his glasses, just as George had left him. He saw George coming in, and looked at him with surprise.

"You here again? I thought I'd seen the last of you," he said menacingly.

"No, you haven't. I am not through telling you all I have to say. And now you will hear me out."

"I hear you. But be quick, and then beat it."

The young barman at the other side of the bar was pouring a liquid from one bottle into another, topping up the bottle, and then moving to the next one.

"When we were in school, I thought the world of you," he said, hoping that his words sounded convincing. "To me, you were the coolest boy I ever met. You were strong, you were funny, all the girls liked you, and the boys respected you. I wanted to be like you, but I was shy, and small and weak. I tried so much to be your friend that it hurt. But you never paid any attention to me. I brought you gifts, and you took them and didn't say 'thanks'. I jumped at your every wish, but you took it for granted. You made me so miserable that on some days I would feel too sick to go to school. So, when you asked me to help you with the test, I refused, because I thought that perhaps now you would pay more attention to me. I hoped that you would understand that also a geek has his value, and that although I was not cool and funny like you, I was worth speaking to, no less than the other boys you used to hang around with.

"Then, one day, you disappeared. I took it that you were so sick and tired of us geeks that you just decided to find something better to do and forget about us. A friend of ours–I forget his name–told me that you were working in that butchers' shop of your uncle's. I came to visit you, but you seemed so powerful in your apron, with the butcher's knife in your hand, that my courage failed me, and I just ran away.

"We all knew you had it in you, and that you would do well, whatever you chose to do. We went on envying you for the whole year–out there with the knife, while we were slaving at useless literature and other boring stuff–and you were the school hero. Then, life went on as life does, and we stopped thinking of you so much, and went on being miserable schoolboys.

"But we never doubted that you would always be the best. Not for a moment. I know you are the best. I have watched you going about your duties as a bartender, proud and strong as ever. The finest bartender I have ever seen. Little wonder that you had no patience for us kids in school. Now, don't you doubt for a second who got the better deal. Not us, not the boys who stayed behind."

"I didn't know," murmured the bartender. "I had no idea that you felt like this. I am sorry if I hurt you. I had no intention." He thought for a few seconds, his chin in his hand, and then asked, "Did you really like me then?"

"I worshipped you. And so did everybody else."

"Well," said the bartender, brightening up, "I guess you are right. I have done quite well, you know? But now, you see, Blond Boy here," he pointed at the young bartender "thinks that he can replace me. But he can't. Nobody can."

"I know, I know. But that's their problem, isn't it?"

"You're right. But I have my professional pride. How can I leave like this? Look at the way he pours drinks." The young bartender was now pouring a beer for a customer, and the glass was filled with froth. "That's no way to treat a drink. That beer is going to be flat. He is ruining the name of this place, you see? This has been going on for months now, since I...had to quit. I don't know what the owners will do now."

"Let them eat cake! Who cares? Only you and I can see the glasses you are cleaning, anyway. Blond Boy's customers get the dirty ones. If they make do with him, why should you pay for it? I don't see why you must be stuck behind this bar, instead of being out and about with me. If you really were my old pal from my school days, we would be out there having fun by now."

The bartender came out from behind the bar, removing his immaculate apron. He put it on the bar and turned to look back. He gave a long look at the bar, the glasses, and the bottles, and then turned his back to them.

"I believe you're right! You are no longer the geek you used to be."

"I take that as a compliment, I think. Well, let's go."

They left the bar and started waking up the street, side by side. Suddenly, they both started laughing, without reason, like children sharing a secret.

"Where are we going, Geek? Do you have any good idea?"

"Well, I know a meadow, not far away from here, and I feel very much like crossing it. Don't you?"

A nod from the bartender was all that was needed. He nodded with a smile, and added from the side of his mouth, "Yeah! Keep walking, Geek, if you know what's good for you."

Meet the Author

Kfir Luzzatto is the author of eleven novels, several short stories, and seven non-fiction books. Kfir was born and raised in Italy and moved to Israel as a teenager. He acquired the love for the English language from his father, a former U.S. soldier, a voracious reader, and a prolific writer. Kfir has a Ph.D. in chemical engineering and works as a patent attorney. He lives in Omer, Israel, with his full-time partner, Esther, their four children, Michal, Lilach, Tamar, and Yonatan, and the dog Elvis.

In pursuit of his interest in the mind-body connection, Kfir was certified as a Clinical Hypnotherapist by the Anglo European College of Therapeutic Hypnosis.

Kfir has published extensively in the professional and general press over the years. For almost four years, he wrote a weekly "Patents" column in Globes (Israel's financial newspaper). His popular guide, *FUN WITH PATENTS—The Irreverent Guide for the Investor, the Entrepreneur, and the Inventor*, was published in 2016. He is an HWA (Horror Writers Association) and ITW (International Thriller Writers) member.

You can visit Kfir's website and read his blog at www.kfirluzzatto.com. Follow him on Twitter (@KfirLuzzatto) and friend him on Facebook (https://www.facebook.com/KfirLuzzattoAuthor/).

www.ingramcontent.com/pod-product-compliance
Lightning Source LLC
Chambersburg PA
CBHW032116170626
46808CB00006B/1971